Acclaim for
A GENIUS BY MOONLIGHT

"A Genius by Moonlight offers a funny and quirky view of the urban angst that forms our lives."

—*Marissa Piesman*

"A Genius by Moonlight is great fun. And Jack Paley is an unusual and appealing detective."

—*Susan Dunlap*

"A Genius by Moonlight gleams with insight and shines with perspicacity. Brady will have to work hard to eclipse this one."

—*Kinky Friedman*

"The genius of *A Genius by Moonlight* is W.J.M. Brady's ability to weave together into a colorful and seamless whole the threads of detective thriller, love story, brainteaser, and—the most vivid part of the tapestry—a vision of paradise lost in irrecoverable youth."

—*Richard Lederer*

An invitation,

in the form of fiction,

to consider nine devious questions

along with one of TV's original

Mental Midgets

A GENIUS
BY
MOONLIGHT

A Novel by
W.J.M. Brady

WASHINGTON SQUARE PRESS
PUBLISHED BY POCKET BOOKS
New York   London   Toronto   Sydney   Tokyo   Singapore

A WASHINGTON SQUARE PRESS *Original* Publication

A Washington Square Press publication of
POCKET BOOKS, a division of Simon & Schuster
1230 Avenue of the Americas, New York, NY 10020

Brady, W.J.M.
    A genius by moonlight: a novel / by W.J.M. Brady.
       p.   cm.
    "A Washington Square Press original publication."
    ISBN 0-671-68558-9
    I. Title.
PS3552.R2455G46   1991
813'.54—dc20   90-12623
                                                        CIP

First Washington Square Press printing February 1991

10 9 8 7 6 5 4 3 2 1

WASHINGTON SQUARE PRESS and WSP colophon are
registered trademarks of Simon & Schuster.

Printed in the U.S.A.

Table of Contents

Chapter One
TRAVEL LIGHT   1

Chapter Two
WHATEVER HAPPENED TO THE MENTAL MIDGETS   29

Chapter Three
THE YEAR OF THE CHAMELEON   51

Chapter Four
THE RIDDLER   70

Chapter Five
MURDER IN WONDERLAND   87

Chapter Six
THE DEAD   120

Chapter Seven
FLOATING ISLAND   140

Chapter Eight
A NIGHT WITH THE HERZOGS   163

Chapter Nine
SHOWTIME   191

Chapter One
TRAVEL LIGHT

WHEN Jack Paley had trouble falling asleep at night, he would lie in bed and run through the periodic table. "Hydrogen, helium, lithium," he would begin, and in his mind the atomic numbers would leap like graceful sheep over fences. "Gallium, germanium, arsenic," he would chant, and by the time Paley had reached his sentimental favorite, einsteinium, which clocked in at atomic number 99, he'd be dead to the world. Sometimes, though, the trick didn't work. And when it didn't, he would wearily sit up in his loft bed, his head almost touching the ceiling, and give in to the idea of being awake for the rest of the night. Out the window, in the buildings across the street, scattered lights revealed scenes from other sleepless lives: the shirtless man ironing endlessly, the determined woman working the oars of a rowing machine, the fashion-plate couple pacing and talking, talking and pacing. In the distance, over the rooftops of SoHo, the word PARK shimmered in blurry orange neon above the entrance to a garage. Sometimes Paley took this word as a divine command, a lightning bolt from the dark Manhattan heavens expressly intended for anyone still awake at this ungodly hour:

Park. Settle down. Get hold of your life. And eventually, if Paley waited long enough, the sun would rise, a gentle persuasion, against all better judgment, that what goes down must come up.

Belinda claimed that Paley's insomniac side was the price of being brilliant, but he dismissed this notion. It was the price of being *human,* he always told her. When you were human, there were nights when you'd be trying to sleep and suddenly you'd become riddled with anxiety. Sometimes Paley would be lying in bed, trying to drift off, when an image of, say, *Ethel and Julius Rosenberg* would instantly click into place, like a slide dropped into a carousel; their faces—Julius's so young and sober, his wife's so homely and terrified—would be with him for the night. All anxiety, Paley had read in a psychology book in college, had to do with fear of death. Certainly you didn't have to be brilliant to worry about death. You didn't have to be brilliant to see *The Seventh Seal* for the third time with the childish hope that maybe this time it would end differently. In the end, Paley knew, Death always won.

Certainly Death had won today.

This morning the temporary employment agency had assigned Paley to be a tour guide on the observation deck of the Empire State Building. It was a rough day to be up so high; everyone in his group held tight to the iron rail and peered over the edge nervously as Paley shouted the staggering statistics of Manhattan life into a stiff wind. He tried to relax the group by telling Fay Wray jokes, but many people weren't listening, and a cluster of Japanese businessmen just looked puzzled.

A combination of gale force winds and vertigo had seized hold of the crowd; mothers held fast to their children's hands, Girl Scouts clung to their berets. Paley sped through his list of facts, summing up both the Garment District and Times Square in a matter of seconds. All he wanted was to be in the elevator, going down. At that moment the wind managed to loosen a newspaper from a businessman's hands. Everyone watched as several sheets soared over the railing and took uneven flight across the city. But many of the pages tumbled across the deck, and these Paley nimbly gathered. Within a few moments, most of the pages had been collected, and he stood helping the grateful man reassemble his paper. It was then that Paley saw it: the obituary of a friend.

"Ex–Child Prodigy, 29, Dies." The item was small, with an accompanying photograph barely bigger than a postage stamp, but still it jumped out at him. The presentation of the facts was as simple and straightforward as Paley's recitation of Empire State Building trivia. The obituary stated that Larry Kelleher had been one of television's Mental Midgets from 1968 to 1975, that he lived with his parents in Burden, New Jersey, and that his death was caused by injuries sustained during a fall in his home. The former quiz kid had worked at various odd jobs, most recently as a "technical consultant," the obituary added, as if his adult life were an afterthought.

Paley stared at the photograph of Larry Kelleher for a long time, bracing the buckling page against the wind, examining the transformed face of his childhood friend. Larry Kelleher didn't look at all the way Paley remembered him: lively and quick-witted and slightly sarcastic. Instead, he looked like someone who haunted convenience stores at night with a Slushie in one hand and a copy of *Jugs* magazine in the other. So this is what it comes down to, Paley thought as he handed the paper back to its owner, folding it at the crease, gently closing the page on Larry Kelleher: two inches of type and an unflattering photo in *The New York Times*.

That night, alone in his loft bed, Paley flipped the pillow to the cool side and pressed his face into it, as though hoping to leave an impression. "The Empire State Building is 1,250 feet tall," he recited to himself, "with the addition of a television antenna bringing the total height to 1,454 feet. It has withstood winds up to 186 miles per hour, and in the highest winds the structure sways slightly." It was no good; the lost face of Larry Kelleher stayed with Paley into the night.

Poor Larry. The obituary had mentioned that a memorial service was planned for the following Saturday, and Paley wondered if any of the other Mental Midgets would be in attendance. He wondered if any of them had made more of their lives than the late Larry Kelleher. Once the Mental Midgets had been the best of friends, a closed circle of like minds that transcended friendship, a team of six that functioned as one. Now they had scattered like so many sheets of newsprint in the wind. In the darkness Paley reached out to the braille clock, a gift given him years before by a blind woman who had hired him to read Ved Mehta novels to her, and ran his fingers across the nubbed surface of the clock's face. *Three A.M.* In just four hours the receptionist from the Fly-By-Night agency would be giving him a wake-up call, sending him out into a world that was suddenly, irrevocably, one Mental Midget shy.

"Candida," he whispered hoarsely into the receiver at seven, "give me something easy." He was lying flat on his back in the loft, his feet hanging over the edge. Sunlight poured through the gates on the window and into the tiny room.

"Rough night?" she said.

"Don't ask." He paused; she seemed to be blowing lightly into the receiver. "What color?" he suddenly said. "Pebble Pink? Cherry Blossom Red?"

"Pardon me?" she asked.

"Your *nails,*" said Paley. "Aren't you putting on nail

4

polish right now, and blowing on it to dry? Isn't that what that sound is?''

Candida laughed again. ''You're too smart for your own good,'' she said. ''Why are you only a temp? You should be running this agency.'' When Paley did not respond, she lowered her voice and said confidentially, ''Sunset Peach. With a coat of Clear.'' Then she rustled through her papers and cleared her throat. ''Okay, here's what I've got for you today,'' she said. At nine A.M., she told him, he was to appear at the stage door of the Algonquin Theater, where a transplanted London musical still in rehearsals was in need of an extra hand. ''I don't know if it will be easy,'' said Candida, ''but it's certainly lower to the ground than yesterday's job.''

''Whatever,'' Paley said. All he wanted, after his sleepless night, was to make it through the workday in one piece. It didn't really matter what was required of him today; today was Tuesday, the one night of the week he spent with Belinda.

He eased himself down the ladder of his loft bed and walked naked into the kitchen, where his claw-footed bathtub sat squarely in the center of the room. Paley opened both taps and let the water roar. He appraised himself in the wavy mirror over the sink, seeing if sleeplessness had altered him at all. But he still looked the same; he almost always did, whether he hadn't slept or had slept like a baby, whether he was thrilled to death or miserable. He looked, women always told him, ''boyish.'' They meant it as a compliment. Paley was twenty-nine, but women always insisted he looked much younger.

''Twenty-three, *max*,'' a woman named Sharon had pronounced that winter over dinner in her cluttered East Village apartment. Her Angora cats had encircled Paley's legs like ankle-cuffs throughout the meal. ''You definitely look twenty-three," she had said. "Just recently out of college."

He had picked at the soba noodles on his plate and said nothing. He might well look twenty-three, he was thinking, but he was long out of college, and he was definitely getting too old for this—whatever *this* was. Dating, sleeping around, sowing his wild oats, or simply making small talk: none of the usual terms quite seemed to cover it. Women responded to his lanky grace, his big head of dark curls, his melancholy, his collection of antique ties, the tricks he could perform with a spoon and a glass in restaurants, the tricks he could perform in bed. He wasn't afraid to purchase diaphragm jelly at drugstores, which, according to these women, some men actually were; he was sentimental about birthdays and Valentine's Day. But he hadn't met anyone who'd really stopped him dead in his tracks until the night he went to a costume party dressed as Edward VIII and met Belinda, who was dressed as Mrs. Wallace Simpson. Even now, though, six months after that night, he still didn't know where they were headed.

Where they were headed. It was strange the way people tended to talk about relationships as though they were *vehicles,* things that could head somewhere or be thrown off track or break down suddenly. But his relationship with Belinda wasn't at all mechanized, was it? he thought. He stood at the mirror, shaving and getting ready for work, and in his peripheral vision he spotted the only real vehicle he possessed: his beloved Braithwaite bicycle, which hung motionless on a rack on the wall.

Paley dressed quickly and carried the collapsible bicycle down the five flights of stairs to the street with one hand, as if the ten-speed were a briefcase. In a way it was: He'd bought it with his first paycheck from Fly-By-Night, and already the lightweight bike had become the reliable fixture of Paley's floating trade, his

Filofax and Rolodex rolled into one. "This is the new me," he'd announced the previous week, modeling the bicycle in the apartment, completely naked but for his wristwatch, while Belinda observed from the loft bed. "My new motto," he had told her, "is 'travel light.' "

"And carry a big stick," she answered, but Paley ignored her. The bike was no joke. It was no luxury, either. In just two weeks it had become part of him, a perfect companion for a commuter who no longer knew from day to day where his work would take him. No more suffocating subway rides crushed against bosoms and attaché cases, no more inhaling a dozen different shades of morning breath and listening to the tinny emanations from a dozen different sets of Walkman headphones. Now, each morning began with Candida from Fly-By-Night tempting Paley in a new direction, and there he'd head, breezing through the streets, squeezing past cars and buses and trucks in a blur of electric blue.

It wasn't that Paley hadn't thought about cultivating a single career. He did most things well, and therein lay the problem: How could he possibly choose among an embarrassment of riches? He would try sitting in an office, but after a few weeks he'd find himself looking out the window at a window in the building across the way, wondering what was going on in that office over *there*. Was the woman at that desk having a better time than Paley? Was her work more important, more interesting?

Paley had traded bonds briefly, taught science to fifth-graders, translated programs from the Italian and the German for the Metropolitan Opera, dispatched food to homeless families who slept in the Port Authority Bus Terminal, but he never stayed at any job for a significant length of time. When the solution to what he should do with his life finally came, it was so staggeringly simple that he was shocked; it reminded him of those "deceptively" simple Zen koans he had studied during his Buddhism seminar at college: "To get to the nut, you must first remove the shell" or "The dog barks; the cat purrs."

There was the nut, right inside the shell; there was the dog and there was the cat: He didn't have to do any one thing, he realized; he could do several things. He could be a temporary employee; he could work at a job until it bored him, and then he could move on. A month before, Paley had signed on with Fly-By-Night, an agency specializing in meeting the needs of businesses that had unusual requests. The work both held Paley's interest and paid the rent on his fifth-floor walk-up apartment in SoHo, and that was enough for now. Still, the irony of his being a temp wasn't lost on him. Every morning when the agency called him with his assignment, Paley remembered the way the "Mental Midgets" show used to begin, with the announcer saying in his oleaginous voice, "And here they are, ladies and gentlemen . . . tomorrow's surgeons and senators and rocket scientists!"

And *now* here they were—one of them dead, another a temp with a brand-new bike. On the sidewalk outside his building Paley unfolded the Braithwaite and studied the river of red brake lights flowing up Sixth Avenue. Paley decided that he had a choice: He could let the death of Larry Kelleher follow him through the day, or he could do what he always did: greet the demands of a new job with open arms and boundless curiosity. Paley swung a leg over the bike, balanced himself on its hair-trigger pedals, and made it to Times Square in twelve minutes, without looking back once.

The stage door of the Algonquin Theater, which Paley now opened, had once been opened by Richard Burton, by Lunt and Fontanne, and by most of the Barrymores.

Paley felt compelled to pause on the threshold for a moment, his eyes closed in silent tribute, before wheeling his bicycle through. He felt giddy as he walked down the dim passage, which smelled—at least to someone with a lively imagination—like ancient greasepaint and wonderfully mildewed costumes. The gears of his bike ticked quietly beside him; in the distance he could hear a woman's easy laughter.

There was something about the theater, he knew, that generated excitement, that allowed people to break into laughter at nine A.M. even if their lives were falling apart. *Especially* if their lives were falling apart.

At college, Paley had briefly, dopily considered a career in the theater. He didn't remember much of college; he had started sneaking gin from his parents' lowboy at the age of fourteen, the year the "Mental Midgets" went off the air, and he stayed drunk, more or less, until after his Harvard graduation, when he checked himself into one of those drying-out places in Arizona. By the time he left the desert he was sober and sad and fully grown-up with no recollection of much of the preceding decade. Still, a few memories remained intact: alarmingly vivid images that sometimes made him stop and wonder what he could possibly have been thinking of. His experience in the theater was one such memory. He had starred as Stanley Kowalski in a musical tribute called *Tennessee, Anyone?;* he'd even garnered good notices in the *Crimson* for his first-act showstopper, "A Fella for Stella."

But *this* was the pinnacle of an actor's career; this was Broadway. In the distance someone played a chromatic scale and Paley felt a swell of something: regret, excitement, nostalgia? Perhaps a combination of all three. He chained his bike to a stanchion in an empty dressing room and walked out onto the stage, his back as straight as a dancer's. Looking up into a flood of yellow light, he squinted at the ancient flies and catwalks and weights that had assisted in a million acts of theatrical legerdemain.

Now they were being put to use in a production of *Women Who Love Too Much: The Musical.* This morning the company was engaged in an intricate number dedicated to the five stages of grief; Paley reported to the harried, motherly stage manager, who sent him to work in the wings, helping the dancers in and out of the sequined costumes for each stage—orange for anger, green for bargaining, and so on, culminating in the white of acceptance. Paley never got a chance to see much of the number, but between the hammering of the pianist on the upright and the complaints of the dancers while they zippered and held their breaths and squeezed, Paley gathered that the sequence hadn't worked to the director's satisfaction in London, and it still wasn't working.

From where Paley was standing, he could glimpse the director, Martin Rotman, a short man with a shaved head and a safari jacket who stood in the third row with his arms folded, pleading with everyone to try to look just a touch more wounded. Little improvement was noted, and ultimately Rotman had everyone break for lunch half an hour early. While much of the cast and all of the crew headed out to the overpriced corner deli, Paley hung back and crept out to the theater lobby. Earlier he'd noticed the wide staircase at the back of the theater, its plum-colored carpet leading down to the lobby, its sleek brass banister just waiting for someone to slide down it. Paley observed the incline along the banister, then perched on the edge.

The slide was effortless, a gift of gravity, a single long glide by the seat of his pants down the center of the stairway. The landing was no less graceful, and he dismounted easily, his face flushed, and bowed low to the empty lobby. "Thank you," he said in his best

Katharine Hepburn voice. "Thank you, each and every one of you. You're too kind."

Then he heard laughter. It was the same laugh he'd heard when he'd arrived at the theater that morning. He looked to the left and saw that it was Andie Sparrow, the star of the show. He'd seen the British pop singer on album covers and awards shows, and from time to time that morning he'd glimpsed her backstage, but this was his first chance to see her at such close range. Her flame-colored hair was pulled back by a simple black headband. She was wearing her rehearsal clothes—an old Beatles sweatshirt and hot-pink leg warmers—and she was sitting on a bench, smoking a cigarette.

"Very nice," she said in a clipped English accent. "Can you do the speech from *Stage Door*?"

Paley felt himself blush violently, but still he proceeded. "The calla lilies are in bloom . . . ," he started, but then he faltered. "That's all I know," he said.

"That's all anyone knows," said Andie Sparrow. They smiled at each other, a strange, complicit smile, as though already they shared some intimate secret.

"I'm Jack Paley," he said tentatively. "I thought I was alone."

"Obviously."

"Was it the most embarrassing thing on earth?" he asked.

"No," she said simply. "It was rather sweet. Your . . . descent was swift, and your impression was decent. What more can a girl want?" She took a long drag. "You won't tell anyone?" she said.

"Pardon me?"

She waved the cigarette toward Paley. "If Martin saw me sneaking a fag, he'd send me packing on the next plane back to London."

"I doubt that."

"You don't know Martin Rotman," she said.

"No, I don't. Actually, it's my first day on the job."

She tilted her head, sizing him up. "And what job might that be?" she said.

"I help women slip into something less comfortable."

She nodded, took a drag, exhaled lightly. "That's right," she said, "I think I saw you off to one side there, lurking among the bodices. So, this is your first job in the theater."

"Does it show that badly?" he asked.

She laughed lightly, tamping out her cigarette in the mound of sand in a standing ashtray. "No," she said, "not at all, in fact. I'm sure you're quite the professional. Averting your eyes at all the right moments, trying not to stare if a stray breast should happen to pop out. A real gentleman."

"Thanks," he said. "I guess."

"It's a compliment. The world could always use another gentleman. But I did notice you haven't run off to lunch with the others. You're not down at the corner *deli,* as you Americans call it, trying to figure out who can help you get your next job in the theater. Therefore," she said, "you're clearly not *in the theater,* as we say."

Paley laughed. "What are you, some kind of detective?"

"No," she said. "Just someone else who's not in the theater."

The conversation, Paley realized, had reached a dizzying point of no return. He tried to think of something to say, something to ask her, but all he could come up with were questions of such drumming triteness that it hurt his head just to dismiss them: How do you like New York? Or: So, do you miss London? Or: What color is your hair in the dark?

"I like New York," Andie said, "but I miss London."

Paley was dumbfounded. For a moment he had to ask himself if he'd somehow gone into a trance and spoken his thoughts without realizing it.

"*You* know," she said, "the friends, the accents, the food."

The food? British cuisine, Paley had always thought, was an oxymoron; everything seemed to be aswim in a white sauce, or accompanied by kippers, but he kept his opinion to himself. He knew what it was like to be the stranger in a strange land; he thought of his first morning at the rehab clinic, when he'd walked, dazed, into the TV room, and a dozen heads had swiveled up from "The Price Is Right" to appraise the newest alcoholic in their midst. He shivered, remembering.

"So, you're alone here?" he asked. "None of your friends with you?"

Andie paused, as though about to say something, then shook her head. "I'm the only one who made it over. Martin thinks the London cast would sound too British to fool an American audience on Broadway," she said. "Even though I'm as British as the changing of the bloody *guard,* I guess he's willing to overlook that little fact because I'm a so-called name. But I'm the only Brit allowed. I had to leave all my friends back in the West End."

"Well," Paley said hesitantly, "he's got a point."

She looked at him. "You think so?"

"Sure," he said. "There's a whole history of actors putting on accents that just don't work. Remember that Proust movie *Swann in Love,* with Jeremy Irons and Ornella Muti talking in crummy French accents? He's British and she's Italian, and the whole thing was so *transparent.* Not everyone can be as talented as Meryl Streep, Ambassador to the World. So Martin Rotman's probably right," he continued. "When Americans do British accents, there's bound to be a minor slip. One second you're in London, the next you're back in some minuscule theater in Greenwich Village, watching a part-time waiter pretend he's the Earl of . . ." Here Paley fumbled for a word. "Chichester," he finished.

Andie laughed that pleasing laugh. "You think so?" she said again.

"I know so," said Paley. "Or at least I think I do. But you don't sound so convinced."

Andie shrugged. Then she looked past Paley, up the stairs and toward the theater.

"Well," she said, "I hate to disappoint you, but you're not quite the expert you think you are. I shouldn't be saying this; I don't want to get anyone in trouble. But I can trust you with a secret, can't I?"

"Me? I'm a gentleman, remember?"

She nodded her head quickly, eager to get on with her revelation. Then she said, in a subdued voice, "There's an impostor here."

"An impostor?" Paley said.

She nodded her head again, closing her eyes. "Martin Rotman has snuck in a British, shall we say, *import*— other than myself—without alerting Customs." Paley looked puzzled. "He's hired an actor from the London cast," Andie explained. "He says it's a matter of principle, of not letting some American actors' union push him around with hiring quotas. I say it's a matter of money. Martin Rotman isn't just the director. He's the producer, too, and these are his pounds being spent here."

"This actor is in the company?" Paley asked.

"You've probably spoken to him."

Paley thought back on all the short, frantic conversations he'd had that day. It could have been anybody.

"But how?" Paley said. "Isn't that incredibly risky?"

"Indeed," she said. "But this particular actor is a master of disguises. Fancies himself a young Olivier, even if he's an *unknown* Olivier. He's studied at the Royal Shakespeare Academy and he sees it as a challenge. You'd never ever guess he wasn't a fine, upstanding, pork-rind-eating American male."

14

"Well, I'm impressed," Paley said.

The distant call of "Places, everyone" told them that the company had returned from lunch. Paley and Andie both glanced up the stairs, then back at each other. Paley was sorry that their time together was over. What were the chances that he would ever again be alone with Andie Sparrow? He had only one more day left at this job, and then he would be off somewhere else. Time would pass, and his brief moment with Andie Sparrow would begin to seem unreal, and he might wonder if it had ever taken place. And surely Andie would forget about him. To her, he was sure, he was just someone to kill a lonely lunch hour with, a friendly voice in a sea of bland accents.

"I think I can pick out your impostor," Paley said. "The fact is, I was an actor, once. And I mean *once*," he quickly added. "One show. Back in college."

She regarded him. Paley wanted to explain more, about *Tennessee, Anyone?* and even about his stint with the Mental Midgets, but how would any of his experiences compare with the career of Andie Sparrow, a woman who lived a life he couldn't even begin to imagine? Besides, he figured, a little mystery about himself couldn't hurt. Nor could a little intellectual muscle-flexing.

Perhaps it was the lingering knowledge of Larry Kelleher's death that reminded Paley now of how every "Mental Midgets" broadcast ended. For most of the show the kids would race one another to recite arcane facts or retrieve obscure trivia. But then, in the final moments of the program, they would be given one last challenge that would cast them into a collective silence. It always seemed impossible at first, but most of the time, during the break for a brief word from the sponsor, one of the kids would rise to the occasion and divine the answer to that week's Extra Credit Question.

"Tomorrow," he said in a stage whisper. "At lunch.

I'll meet you here. Bring several men with you, a few Americans and the impostor. Tell them you want me to meet them, that I just love meeting actors. And I bet I'll be able to find your man."

"You're on," Andie said, and she flashed him a wicked smile. "But we have to make it an honest wager. If I'm right, then you and I will go out for a night on the town."

"And if *I'm* right?"

She studied him through narrow eyes. "Then you and I will go out for a night on the town."

Paley laughed, shaking his head. "My, what a wide variety of choices," he said. "I don't know about this."

"Unless, of course," Andie Sparrow added, "you have a wife."

"I didn't say that."

"A girlfriend, then. A boyfriend."

"I didn't say that, either."

"So you're unattached."

Paley folded his arms. "How can you tell? You see, you *are* a detective."

"No," she said. "Just a wishful thinker." And then, before he could respond, or even drop open his mouth in dumb surprise, she skipped up the stairway, two steps at a time, sliding her right hand along the same banister that minutes earlier had brought them together.

But the fact was, Paley did have Belinda. And if they weren't attached, exactly, then he wasn't sure what they were. What did you call someone with whom you spent one ecstatic night a week, someone in whose arms you awoke every Wednesday morning? This was a problem that lately had plagued both Paley and Belinda, a minor question of semantics that sooner or later seemed to worry everyone of marriageable age in this brutal city. Still, he knew what Andie Sparrow meant about his being unattached, and he knew what *he* had meant about being unattached, and he knew that the two meanings didn't match.

Paley spent the rest of the afternoon at the theater laboring under the vague suspicion that he had somehow misled Andie about that crucial fact. No, it was more than a suspicion; as Belinda herself had taught Paley, he had an addiction to flirting. He had given up drinking years before, and with the help of periodic, crack-of-dawn AA meetings and occasional screenings of *The Lost Weekend,* he had never fallen on his old ways, but since then he had taken up other avocations in its place. And flirting was one of them.

Paley wasn't sure what, if anything, was wrong with flirting, but Belinda always insisted that flirtation was verbal foreplay, and that if it wasn't consummated, it could only lead to disappointment. And if it *was* consummated—well, she didn't want to know about it. "But that's just it," Paley had told her. "Flirting is safe sex." He flashed her a winning smile, but she was not moved. A series of tense, unresolved conversations like this first gave him the idea that they shouldn't rush into anything, that they should try spending the night together only once a week. And so far their system worked: On Tuesday night they were always ready for each other, always giddy with anticipation by the time eight o'clock arrived.

But tonight there was so much going on inside him that he didn't know what to focus on. His thoughts led first to Belinda, then to Andie Sparrow, then to the sad death of Larry Kelleher, and back again in an unending circle. As he carried his Braithwaite up the stairs to his apartment after work, he felt burdened by much more than the few pounds of aluminum.

Paley stopped for a moment on the second-floor landing and inhaled. The building was an even mix of elderly

Italian widows and twenty-year-old performance art-
ists with names like Bullet and Jujube. On this floor he
could smell tomatoes and onions simmering; one flight
up it was strictly turpentine and Thai stick. When he
reached the fifth floor, his floor, old Mrs. Cellini opened
her apartment door an inch or two and asked, "Paley?
Is that you?"

"Yes, it's me," he answered.

"Then here goes," she said.

He looked into the crack at the door and saw a pair of
ancient eyes staring out from the darkness of her
apartment.

"Shoot," he said.

"In what year did the Tudor period end?" she asked
him in her meek little voice.

"Sixteen oh three," he answered swiftly.

"Bravo!" said Mrs. Cellini.

It happened like this every night. Mrs. Cellini never
missed his return, and never failed to fire a question at
him. Paley always got it right. She had been so thrilled
when he had moved into the building; years before, she
said, she had watched Paley faithfully on Tuesday evenings, as he and the other five panelists sat in caps and
gowns behind their tiny school desks on the set of
"Mental Midgets." Paley was surprised that she'd recognized his name; as the years passed, people still seemed
to recall the show fondly, but most had forgotten the
names of the individual Midgets. They might remember
"the funny one" or "the pretty one" or "the tall one"
(that was Paley), but usually nothing more. Back then,
though, Paley had been many viewers' favorite Midget.

By the time he was twelve, Paley had received love
letters from thousands of moony, myopic girls ("I hope
you won't think it too forward of me to write, but I was
so impressed by your answer about Georgian architec-
ture this week!!!! Plus, you're really cute!!!"), several

scholarship offers from colleges he'd never heard of ("On behalf of Mullins State University, I would like to invite you to matriculate in the fall as the youngest student in Mullins history . . ."), and hate mail from parents ("Our son Philip knows twice as much as you and yet isn't it ironic that you're on TV and he's still an unknown").

But then the Midgets reached that awkward age when voices began to crack and complexions started to erode, and suddenly those geniuses no longer seemed quite so adorable. The ratings faltered, and the show was taken off the air, replaced in its time slot by a sitcom about a suburban white family that adopts a set of Chinese triplets. Years went by; Paley grew up, his hair darkened and his skin roughened. He took up jogging and muscles developed in his long arms and legs. Now he was twenty-nine, and nobody ever recognized him on the street. Sometimes, when his name was said aloud, another person in the room would ask if he was possibly Jack Paley the Mental Midget—but only sometimes. Actually, in the past few years, it had happened exactly twice. The sole vestige of Paley's Midget self was his height; he had been tall for a twelve-year-old, and now he was tall for a twenty-nine-year-old. The child was gone, and in his place stood a man whose mail consisted of the kinds of things he'd pulled from the box today—a wedding announcement from a college roommate, pleas for donations from Sally Struthers and Danny Thomas, and a circular from Moe Schlosser's Big Man's Shop.

"Would you like to come in for some refreshments?" Mrs. Cellini asked.

"No thanks," Paley said. He knew very well that his neighbor probably hadn't had guests since the McCarthy era. "I've got company tonight."

"Okay, dear," said Mrs. Cellini. "Have fun." She closed her door and triple-bolted it.

Company. Was it all right to call Belinda company? He wasn't sure. Inside his apartment, the answering machine was blinking twice in rapid succession. Paley played back his messages. The first call was from a woman he had flirted with while warming up for a run in Central Park months before, and who occasionally made up excuses to call him.

"Hi there," she said. "It's Jean." Pause, giggle. "Jean Sandberg, you dope. I was just thinking last night about how you said you liked lobster. Because I saw that there's a new seafood place in my neighborhood and they have a lobster special. I thought of you immediately when I saw the sign."

Paley squinted. Lobster made him break out in hives. He didn't know what she was talking about. The next message was from his mother.

"Hello, dear," she said in a slow, loopy voice that indicated she'd called during cocktail hour: anytime after nine in the morning. "I just wondered if you'd seen the papers about poor Leo—no *Larry*—Kelleher's death. It's just so sad, so darn sad." Then there was a crash, the receiver obviously slipping to the ground. Paley could hear fumbling, then his mother's voice once again. "Whoopsy," she said. "I'm just an old butterfingers. As I was saying, honey, it's so sad about that boy. . . . I remember how much he knew about classical languages. Oh, I guess life's like that sometimes." There was silence for about five seconds, then something that almost sounded like faint crying, and then she hung up.

His mother left messages like this once a week; usually the next day his father called to apologize. Paley sighed and rewound the tape. It was already six-thirty; he had to get moving. He submerged himself in the bathtub in the kitchen, his white knees rising before him. He could never take a bath without wondering about the immigrants who had settled this neighborhood more than a century before, and how much shorter they must have been. He lay as comfortably as he could in the bath until it dropped down to room temperature, and then he climbed out, spattering water across the linoleum like the family dog. To get himself going, Paley put on his favorite Talking Heads album and did a loose-limbed dance across the room, his arms and legs and towel flapping. When the song ended, he dried himself off, then unscrewed the top from the bottle of cologne that Belinda had given him the week before. It smelled just like wood shavings. Instead of Evanescence, they should have named it Gerbil Cage or Timber! Still, he didn't want her to be hurt, so he swatted a little behind his ears and into the tangles of hair under his arms.

A little later Belinda arrived, and even before she'd taken off her coat, Paley was planting a dotted line of kisses along her neck. She didn't object. She backed him against the wall under a shelf of saucepans and colanders and salad spinners and began to open the buttons of his shirt. In a moment he was completely naked and she was still completely dressed.

"There," she said in a breathy voice, "a slightly altered version of my favorite work of art: *Déjeuner sur l'Herbe.*"

Eventually they made it into the loft bed, from which Belinda's coat was dropped to the floor along with the rest of her clothes. Paley inhaled her expensive Swiss shampoo and she inhaled his wood shavings. There was a thrilling urgency to the whole situation, as though it had been two years since the previous Tuesday.

"I feel like a convict on a conjugal visit," Paley said.

Belinda laughed. Her laugh was staccato, very different from Andie Sparrow's. It chilled him, that he was thinking about another woman's laugh right now, even fleetingly. But in a moment, Belinda ran her face along his neck, whispering to him in a language that seemed not quite English, not quite Latin, not quite pig latin, and he forgot all about Andie, all about everything.

Later, when Belinda climbed down the ladder to throw a little water on her overheated face, Paley leaned over the side and whispered, "There. A slightly altered version of *my* favorite work of art: *Nude Descending a Staircase.*" She smiled, and Paley followed her down. While Belinda washed, he took a couple of eggs from the refrigerator and whisked them together in a bowl with some Worcestershire sauce and a handful of herbs from a little clay pot that she had brought back from France. She was always *giving* him things, he realized. If it weren't for Belinda, the only thing he would own would be his Braithwaite. Belinda finished washing up and Paley made omelets. They ate sitting side by side in the loft bed with the lights off. The only light came from the street, and the only sound—except for their conversation and the gentle scraping of forks on plates—also came from the street, where cars honked and people shouted. But it all seemed to be coming from another city somehow, another island. Up here in their aerie in a tower above the street, Paley leaned against Belinda's shoulder and sighed in that end-of-the-day way.

"Tired?" she asked. He nodded. "Insomnia last night?" she asked. He nodded again. "You could have called me, you know," she said. "I just might have come over and sung you to sleep. Brahms' 'Lullaby' or 'Twinkle Twinkle, Little Star' or 'Honky Tonk Women.' "

Paley shook his head. He'd actually thought about calling her. He *had* entertained the idea of riding his bike in the middle of the night uptown to her West Seventy-Third Street brownstone apartment, where he would have hammered a finger on the buzzer downstairs and begged to be let up. But it had been Monday. For all he knew, Belinda might have been with another man; it wasn't likely, but it *was* possible. Anything was. She and this mystery man might have been making love, or worse yet, sitting in bed watching old movies and eating sesame noodles. And that would have been unbearable to witness: the white Chinese take-out containers scattered on the night table, the chopsticks suggestively crossed on a plate, the television showing Fred MacMurray and Barbara Stanwyck getting hot for each other.

"We made a pact," he said.

"Well, it was your idea, and it's a stupid pact," she said. "It's right out of a magazine in a gynecologist's waiting room: 'How to Spend Less Time with Your Boyfriend and Love It.' "

"I know," he said sheepishly. "It's just that I hate objectifying what we are," he said. "You know. 'Boyfriend.' 'Girlfriend.' It all sounds so silly."

"How about 'mate'?" she said. "No, that makes us sound Australian."

"Or like sailors," said Paley. "And I don't think I could call you 'my woman' without thinking of Catfish Row."

"So what does that leave us?" she said. " 'Significant other'?"

"Well, there's always 'fuck buddy,' " he said.

"Now *that* I can live with," said Belinda. "Just think: You'll come home with me to my parents' house in Locust Valley, and I'll say, 'Mumsy, Dadsy, I'd like you to meet Jack Paley, my *fuck buddy.*' "

"It wouldn't go over big in Locust Valley?" Paley murmured.

"No," said Belinda.

"Then what about 'womanfriend'?" he asked. "Or 'manfriend'?"

She rolled her eyes. "Nice try," she said. "No, what we have . . . defies definition."

"Yeah, that's it," he said. "A love like no other."

"True originals," said Belinda. "We wrote the book of love." She put down her plate and ran long, beautiful fingers with incongruously bitten nails through his hair. "Seriously, though," she said, "why couldn't you sleep?"

" 'Why I Couldn't Sleep Last Night,' by Jack Paley," he said, then paused. "Troubles."

"What kind?"

"Death."

"The usual," said Belinda. She shook her head and her blond hair fell across her breast, and he had to look away or he was sure he'd become too excited. They still had a lot of talking to do. Belinda couldn't stand it when Paley didn't sleep. Sleep, according to Belinda Frank, was God's greatest gift. Sometimes, she told him, she slept for twelve to thirteen hours, and once when she was a child, she had been so deeply, happily asleep that her parents were convinced she had dropped into an irreversible coma.

"No, not the usual," Paley said. He quickly told Belinda about Larry Kelleher's death. She listened in silence, and then he was silent, and then she said, "That's rough."

Paley nodded.

"I'd like to go with you to the memorial service," she said. "If that's okay."

Paley shook his head. "Thanks, really. But I'd rather go alone."

She gave him a level look. "Ah," she said, "the old inscrutable bond of the Midgets."

He said nothing. It was difficult to explain, being part of something like that, something that had defined him and then consumed him and then ended badly, like a relationship. Besides, if he started seeing Belinda whenever he wanted, he would be seeing her every night. He loved all things about her—her smart-mouthed wit, her blond skin and matching hair, the way she looked wearing his Harvard crew jacket and nothing else. But he couldn't, or wouldn't, allow himself to start relying on Belinda, because where would that leave him—the new Jack Paley, the one who travels light?

They sat for a while longer in the darkness, with the remnants of two omelets rapidly cooling and hardening, and finally they put the plates aside. Tucked in beside her, his hand curving on her clavicle, her hand settled at the base of his spine, Paley whispered, "Belinda? You don't really call your parents Mumsy and Dadsy, do you?" But she was already asleep.

" 'Fear of Commitment,' front and center," Martin Rotman announced the next morning from the third row of the Algonquin, and instantly the company mobilized, like a flight crew scrambling under a sneak attack. Paley didn't see Andie until she emerged from the opposite wing at the precise moment she was to deliver the first note of her solo. But she glanced his way, found him in the wings, and nodded a discreet greeting. The wager, she seemed to be saying, was still on.

All morning Paley eavesdropped on the actors. The impostor was good, he had to admit; Paley couldn't pick him out. By the lunch break he was almost ready to concede defeat, if only to let Andie know that the game had gone far enough. Paley rode the banister to the bottom of the stairs and waited. He tried to think of what to say to her. He didn't want to mislead her, to make her think he was *unattached*. Because he wasn't—was he?

As they had agreed, Andie showed up with three men.

"I told you that I'd formally introduce you to some of the cast," said Andie pointedly, "so here they are."

"Pleased to meet you," Paley said. "It must be so exciting to be in a Broadway show." Andie rolled her eyes.

She couldn't have picked more different physical types if she'd tried; and clearly she *had* tried, Paley thought. She was taking this little game very seriously. So he would, too, he decided. He'd deal with the matter of Belinda later on.

"Jack Paley, this is Gerald," Andie said, "as in 'I Need My Space.' "

"Ah," said Paley, thinking of the solo in act two. "You're the tenor."

"Yep," said Gerald. "Pleased to meet you."

"And this," Andie said, "is David."

A short man with dark hair worn in a brush-cut stepped forward.

"Pleased to meet you," said Paley.

"Likewise to you, too," David said.

"And finally," said Andie, "this is James."

A redhead whose onstage footwork Paley had admired extended his hand. "You're working costumes in the wings, right?" James asked. Paley nodded. The group of five stood in an awkward circle, gossiping about the director, the show, and jobs. When the call came from inside the theater for everyone to return to the stage, they broke up quickly. Paley and Andie walked a few feet ahead of the men toward the stairs.

"So?" she whispered. "What's your verdict, Mr. Linguistics?"

He shook his head. "I can't do this," he said.

"You disappoint me," said Andie. "I had you figured for being a lot smarter than that. Especially as you were so sure of yourself. But if you can't do it—"

"I didn't mean I *couldn't* do it," Paley whispered. But before he had a chance to say that what he meant was that he *shouldn't* be doing *this*—shouldn't be betting over a night out with her, shouldn't be misleading her about being unattached, shouldn't be encouraging any development he wasn't willing to follow through on—she said softly but intensely, "Then do it."

Paley looked at all three men again.

"I'm sorry, I can't," he said, and he sprinted ahead to the stairs. Well, he thought, that was certainly a quick flirtation, and it hadn't led anywhere; Belinda would be proud. But as he climbed the stairs, he felt compelled to explain to Andie, to say something about his skittish behavior. Before he reached the top he glanced back over his left shoulder, where she was lost in conversation with David about the "Abandonment Blues" number.

Suddenly Paley leaned over the banister. "I have something to tell you," he whispered to her. "Alone."

Gerald and James threw each other significant glances, then discreetly stepped around Paley and continued up the stairs. Andie turned to David and told him she'd catch up. The three men disappeared together up the aisle.

"Well," she said to Paley, "this odd behavior of yours certainly should keep the company pleasantly swimming in gossip for weeks to come." She stood with her hand on her hip.

"I can explain," he said. But Paley didn't know where to begin. That he was attracted to her but that they couldn't see each other? That he had only been flirting? That he was attached? That he was unattached but unwilling? He didn't know what to say.

And then he did.

"I know who your Englishman is," he said.

The Extra Credit Question is:

How Did Paley Know?

(Solution on next page)

ʃolution

Andie raised an eyebrow. "Do tell," she said.

"The accents were all certainly flawless," said Paley, "but the import is probably David."

"Touché," said Andie softly. "A good guess. What did he say that gave him away?"

"It's not what he said," said Paley. "It's what he *did*. When we were climbing the stairs a second ago, three of us stayed to the right of the banister, but two of us—you and David—*stayed to the left*. David may have the American accent down pat," Paley said, "but he still walks the way you Brits drive. Always on the left."

Andie took hold of Paley by his shirt collar and pulled him close, against the banister that still separated them. The brass wedged into his waist. He was afraid that she was going to kiss him, right there under the EXIT sign, and that he would be unable to resist. But all she said was, "So what are you, some kind of detective?"

Chapter Two
WHATEVER HAPPENED TO THE MENTAL MIDGETS

$\int$O these were the friends of Larry Kelleher. It was a motley crew that mounted the steps of St. Christopher's on the day of the memorial service. Paley stood for a moment before the cathedral in his raincoat on this overcast morning, surveying the crowd, trying to ascertain what sort of person little Larry Kelleher had become.

The sort, Paley remembered from the obituary, who lived with his parents. Larry had grown up in this neighborhood, near Columbia University, the only son of old lefties. As a boy Paley had been invited only once to the Kellehers' brownstone on 116th Street; the occasion, he recalled, was a May Day party, a nervous afternoon of Pete Seeger singalongs and noncompetitive parlor games. Paley remembered Larry Kelleher's father as a burly source of boomed opinions, his mother as a caftanned spirit bearing brownies; they loomed over the party, and they lingered in Paley's memory as huge figures, inflated with the vigor of self-assurance. Now, when Paley found them in the crowd on the steps of St. Christopher's and offered his condolences, they seemed shrunken by more than age; their confidence was gone, their faces sagged with confusion more than grief, as if they were trying to imagine what had gone wrong. Hadn't they raised a brilliant son? Hadn't they surrounded him with all the privileges of a vital university community? Hadn't they educated him in the proper politics? Hadn't they taught him "This Land Is Your Land"—all nine verses—before he could even read? Was it the move to the suburbs, their one concession to complacency, that had doomed Larry? If they'd stuck it out, battled the collapse of the city with their fervor of old instead of joining the migration to the suburbs beyond the Hudson River, would that have saved their son? Whatever happened to little Larry, the Mental Midget?

These were good questions. If they weren't necessarily the questions haunting Mr. and Mrs. Kelleher on this terrible day, they certainly were the questions nagging at Paley. It was difficult to learn much from the crowd on the steps; among the mourners was the usual assortment of middle-aged men in gray business suits who looked like uncles and middle-aged women in plastic rain bonnets who looked like aunts. But there was another element here as well: a small population of nervous-looking types in their late twenties. Paley noticed one man in particular; slowly climbing the cathedral steps, he took a few last puffs of a cigarette before crushing it underfoot on the white, unblemished stone. This wasn't your usual place-of-bereavement behavior.

The man approached. He wore a shiny gray suit with wide lapels. His eyes darted all about before he slipped into the darkness of the cathedral.

"Davy," Paley suddenly called. The man turned and stepped back out into the daylight. It was he: Davy Herzog, always considered the wild card among the Midgets. Poor paranoid Davy, who never seemed to take pleasure in being "gifted," who always looked as though he imagined someone might take his plate away at any moment. Paley hadn't seen Davy Herzog in fif-

teen years, and although the change in him was startling, Paley couldn't say that he was surprised.

Herzog was a living illustration of the word *burnout*.
He turned a pair of narrow eyes to Paley, and after a
moment he opened his mouth so a final curl of smoke
could roll out. "Hey hey, Jack Paley," he said in a
familiar voice. From this threatened and threatening-
looking man emanated the voice of a prepubescent boy
boasting about his mineral collection.

The two men awkwardly shook hands. "I wondered if
I'd see you," Paley said.

"Why?" said Herzog. "Who told you I'd be here?"

"No one, no one," said Paley. "I just thought, you
know, that some of the old crowd would show. I don't
know where anyone lives, or who had heard Larry had
died. I didn't know who could make it."

"Or who would *want* to make it," said Herzog. "Those
weren't exactly the greatest years of anyone's life." He
paused and corrected himself. "I mean, they *were* the
greatest years," he said. "That's the problem."

Paley nodded briefly. He knew what Herzog meant; it
had been the sentiment he himself had carried with him
for years, but had never been able to explain fully to
anyone else. Sometimes, during one of his bouts of
insomnia, Belinda would make him talk about it. So
Paley would sit up in his loft bed, trying to explain.
Belinda always listened well, nodding, her head tilted
slightly, but there was no way she could have really
gotten it. Because she wasn't one of *them*. This must be
the way the Kennedys felt, he thought. You were either
inside the compound or outside.

But there was no Kennedy-like glamour associated
with the Mental Midgets. It had all happened too many
years ago, and the world, not to mention television, had
changed astonishingly since then. Who would want to
watch a bunch of brainy kids in caps and gowns raising

their hands to answer trivia questions when instead they could watch underdressed women writhing to thumping music at any time of day or night? But these grown-up prodigies would carry their Mental Midget histories to the grave. One of them already had. *Once I was somebody*, Paley sometimes thought. *Once I was special. But now I am just like everyone else.* But maybe not just like everyone else. Maybe not like *anybody* else, Paley thought, because as he glanced over Herzog's shoulder and out into the crowd, he realized that the shifty types, the nervous-looking people he had noticed arriving at the cathedral, were, one and all, Mental Midgets coming to pay their respects. They weren't special anymore; now they were just *odd*.

Even as he watched, Olive Herne was making her way up the steps. He saw the way she twisted the edges of her scarf between her fingers, practically shredding the wool. It was in the eyes, and it was in the hands. Restless, as though they could find no place to land.

Just as Olive was about to enter the cathedral, she noticed Paley and Davy watching her. "My God," she said, her voice flat, "pay dirt."

Olive's hair, which as a child she had once worn in a single braid down her back like Pocahontas, now fell in a spray across her shoulders. Her skin was pale as milk. Skim milk, Paley thought. Olive looked great in her black wool coat and a deep-violet scarf. Her hands kept skittering along the scarf's fringe.

"Hello, Olive," Paley said, stepping forward to kiss her cheek. She inclined her face toward him gracefully. He kissed air. Once, in the green room of Studio B, when everyone else was off having lunch, he had actually kissed her mouth and undone her braid. But that was a long time ago. Now she wouldn't even look at him for more than a second. Her eyes jumped all around. "I'm glad you could make it," he said, unsure if this was the truth. He could live without Olive Herne; he had done so for many years.

"Me, too," Olive said. "I just got in yesterday from London. I'm still exhausted, but I felt it was important to come. To pay my last respects."

She and Herzog still hadn't said hello, Paley realized, and he wondered if they recognized each other. Just then, the two of them nodded at each other warily. Herzog leaned over to her and said, in a childish sing-song, "I know a secret about you, Olive. And it's a very *big* secret."

Olive stared at him, eyes widening, and it might have been Paley's imagination, but the color seemed to leave her face for a moment. Before Paley had a chance to wonder what was going on, Tracy Selwyn appeared, looking exactly the same as always. She was small and impish and restless and androgynous. Her fair hair was short all over, except in front, where one forelock hung in her eyes. Three earrings studded one ear. Paley found her attractive in a puzzling way. "Hi, all," she said, and once again the nervous crowd said their nervous hellos. No one seemed to know how to behave; everyone looked ready to bolt.

As Olive and Tracy attempted small talk, Paley pulled Herzog aside. "What was that about," he said, "that thing you said to Olive?"

"Oh, that," said Herzog. "You know Olive's newspaper column?" Paley nodded. Every week a blurred photo of Olive Herne adorned a question-and-answer feature called "The Smartest Woman in the World" in *Cityspeak,* one of those free newspapers that could be found on top of cigarette machines in diner doorways all over downtown Manhattan. "My cousin who works for MTV tells me Olive is going to get her own show," Herzog went on. "He knows I knew her when we were kids. She'll have her own little program every afternoon based on her column. You know: *The Smartest Woman in the World Helps You with Your Homework* kind of thing. But it hasn't been officially announced yet, so *shh,"* and Herzog held a finger to his lips.

Paley nodded. Herzog's warning relieved him of the responsibility of offering Olive his congratulations. Paley always had trouble with social encounters that required a polite lie; the fact was, the couple of times he'd chanced across Olive's column, he had found it more smart-alecky than smart. "What is the highest number in the world?" went one question. "Twenty-nine thousand twenty-eight," was her answer, "which is the height in feet of Mt. Everest. Any higher number would necessarily have to be *out* of this world!"

Still, Paley couldn't be sure that his opinion of Olive's column wasn't tainted by jealousy. After all, she was an old crush—not to mention a Mental Midget who had actually figured out a modest means of capitalizing on her intellect. Well, he'd have to get used to it; certainly Olive would prosper now. In the smudged pages of *Cityspeak,* wedged between ads for video dating and Cajun Night at a local restaurant, the photograph of Olive hardly smoldered. But on television, Paley imagined, the adult Olive would exude a pensive glamour. The harsh lights of a TV studio had always flattered her pale skin, and Olive had always known it. As a Mental Midget she liked to walk the line between Gina Lollobrigida and Hannah Arendt. Now he could imagine her grooming herself as a sex symbol for teenage boys high on hormones: teacher with a whip. Paley wasn't proud of the image of Olive that flashed to mind just then; it was one of those momentary lapses of taste best kept to oneself, like the picture of Princess Diana wrestling in her royal bedchambers, back arched, doe eyes fluttering, that occasionally entered Paley's imagination, uninvited but not easily dismissed.

The last to drift over was Steve Carrera. He was adjusting his tie as he mounted the steps and shrugging his shoulders so that his suit jacket would hang better on his overdeveloped torso. Paley recognized these vain but touching tics from fifteen years before. By the time Steve arrived, the rest of the crowd had already gone inside. Once again, the Mental Midgets were left by themselves, huddling in a small group out in the cold.

"What's the deal?" said Steve by way of greeting. "We just going to stand here?" He looked like a young investment banker who spent all his free time with a personal trainer. But despite the muscled body packed into an expensive suit, there was still that telltale *unsettled* look about the eyes.

None of these people, not one, looked even vaguely happy. An outsider might have attributed this to the sadness of the occasion, but Paley recognized it as something more.

"I wonder," he suddenly said, "about Larry. Do you think he was happy?"

No one spoke. Finally Tracy said, "He never really did anything with his life, I don't think. I was talking to his mother a few minutes ago, and she was telling me things. Like how Larry hadn't gotten his act together. He was trying to do something in computers. But he couldn't find work, and he had no money. He still lived at home."

"That's where he died, right?" said Olive. "In his parents' house?"

Paley nodded. "Does anybody know *how* he died?" he asked warily.

"Fell down the basement stairs," Tracy said. "You know Larry."

He knew Larry. Paley remembered Larry's famous clumsiness on the show: how he'd stumble in his eagerness to sit at his desk, and his mortarboard would remain askew until the first commercial break, or how he'd drop a pencil and it would roll across the set for an agonizingly long time, like a bottle down the aisle of a movie theater.

"He spent a lot of time in the basement," Tracy went on. "That's where he kept his models of World War Two bomber planes. His parents came home one afternoon and found him at the bottom of the stairs. He'd broken his neck."

"That's terrible," said Olive. "What a way to go. *Snap.*" She made a gesture with her hands.

Everyone murmured in agreement.

"The obituary said he worked as a technical consultant recently," Paley said. "What does *that* mean?"

"Oh, you know," said Steve. "A consultant. You rent yourself out to corporations. Wherever anybody needs help. I do some of that myself. The Terrible Twos Toy Company hires me to kind of knock around some ideas once in a while. You know."

"And I've been a consultant to a design firm," offered Tracy.

Paley turned to Herzog, who nodded. "Sure," he said. "Haven't you done any consulting, Paley?"

Paley had to admit that he had, in his own meager way. Only he had never called it anything as fancy as "consulting." He was a *temp,* and that's what he would continue to be, as long as his ambitions were still all over the map. As Paley looked around the circle of Mental Midgets, he felt a deep surge of melancholy. Everyone here was lost, he realized, each in his or her own way. After the television show had gone off the air, the Midgets had been cut loose into the world, armed with small trust funds and heads full of obscure and useless knowledge. In the first year after the cancellation, the Midgets had attempted to socialize with one another, but it was always awkward. Without a set of questions to answer, without hot lights shining in their faces, without a mutual purpose, they had found that all they had in common was the show. And it wasn't enough.

But now, standing before the cathedral, Paley couldn't stop thinking about how much time had passed yet how little any of them had really changed. They were still child prodigies, he realized, because in a peculiar way they were all still *children*. None of them had made a graceful transition into adulthood; all of them still stood uncertainly on the brink. Paley had a strong sense that everyone here would check the "Undecided" box when it came to a career. Even Olive, with her newspaper column and now her upcoming TV show, was still a master of *nothing*. They all knew bits and pieces about various disciplines—lots of bits and pieces—the same bits and pieces they'd known years before. Together they were a solid unit, a Center for Advanced Studies, but individually—and here Paley did a quick scan of the group—individually, they were all a little pathetic. In a way, they had become *Menial* Midgets.

"So we're all consultants," Paley said with a smile. And one by one the other Midgets began to smile, too. The realization seemed to dawn on them collectively. There was not a single surgeon or senator or rocket scientist among them. Not a one. Just a bunch of geeky oddball brainiacs who hadn't channeled their intelligence into anything of note.

"Consultants of the world, unite!" said Tracy. "You have nothing to lose but your . . ." She paused, straining for a punch line.

"Dignity," offered Herzog.

Dignity. It was something that seemed to be lacking from this group. Even Olive Herne, who was beautiful and comported herself accordingly, who was about to rise from their ranks into a respectable career, had an edge of undignified desperation about her.

"So what do you say, are we going to stand here all day?" asked Steve.

They all agreed that it was time to go inside and pay their last respects to Larry, but just as they turned and began walking inside, a voice called out to them: "Wait up! All you Midgets, wait up!"

Paley was startled to see Hal Josephson, known by everyone as "Professor," climbing out of a taxi at the curb and lumbering up the shallow steps. Long ago he'd been a young junior-faculty member of the philosophy department of a small liberal arts college in Pennsylvania who had quit his job to become the Mental Midgets' coach, but now he was middle-aged and overweight and pink faced. Once he had tutored these kids around the clock, shaping the Mental Midgets into a powerhouse of a team; here he was, fifteen years later, slow and bloated. An image flashed through Paley's mind: the Professor sitting in the red vinyl booth of a steak house, doubling over the table with a massive coronary.

When he approached the Midgets now, there was visible emotion in his face. The Professor himself had not been born with "the gift," his term for the brilliance of his young charges. *His* gift, he said (which was *a* gift, not to be confused with *the* gift), was for extracting brilliance from others, coaxing it out delicately, like crabmeat from a claw. He had pulled amazing things out of the Midgets, and viewers and sponsors alike had been thrilled.

"Hey, Professor," Paley said as Hal approached. The two men hugged; the Professor pounded him lightly on the back.

"All of you, in one place," the Professor began, his voice constrained. "Well, almost all of you."

"Yeah, poor Larry," said Steve, somberly nodding his head. Everyone else in the group shifted uncomfortably, except Herzog, who said, "And don't forget Dora."

Dora. Dora Bunyan. The group fell into silence at the mention of her name. It was the first time Paley had thought about her in years; he imagined it must be the same for the rest of the group. Dora Bunyan had been an unsmiling seven-year-old, wide for her age and cursed with crooked teeth; the official reason she was released from the Mental Midgets after the pilot episode was that her intellect wasn't up to the standards set by the others, but nobody believed it. She had answered her questions capably; she had even run the category in Women in History. But she had lacked screen presence. Even as kids the Mental Midgets could figure out that the real reason for Dora Bunyan's dismissal was cosmetic, and when her replacement proved to be the eminently telegenic Olive Herne, there could be little doubt that the Mental Midgets had learned the first important lesson of their show business careers: Life isn't fair. As the show became a runaway hit the vaguely embarrassing memory of Dora Bunyan receded, until at last she was little more than the answer to a trivia question, the Pete Best of the Mental Midgets.

"I *had* forgotten about Dora," said Tracy. "Dora Bunyan. God."

"Whatever happened to her?" said Steve. "Does anybody know?"

Nobody knew. Herzog shrugged. "Whatever happened to any of us?" he said.

"All right, now," said the Professor. "This day is going to be difficult enough without everybody getting maudlin. Let's just try to enjoy our own little reunion here. When I see you together again, I can't tell you . . ."

"Oh, tell us," said Olive.

The Professor looked around the small group. "You know," he began, "my life has been pretty decent since I last saw all of you. I joined the philosophy department at NYU. I teach Hobbes and Locke to bulimic eighteen-year-olds, and it's fine work, really it is. But never," he said, *"never* have I experienced such pure, unadulterated joy as I did when I was your coach. Never have I felt as happy." He licked his lips nervously. "I guess nostalgia is the thing that carries you through your dotage," he said. "At least it is for me. Maybe you kids will be different." Nobody said anything. "Now," he said, suddenly brightening, "I want to hear all about *you*. You're the interesting ones, you're the ones with the high IQs."

"I think IQs go down as you get older, don't they?" said Tracy. "I read that somewhere."

"What a shame," said Steve. "Now we're probably only in the three-figure range."

Suddenly the reminiscing was interrupted by hoofbeats. Everyone turned to find two men coaxing a horse up the cathedral steps.

"Come on, girl," one of the men was saying. "Come on." The white mare hung back and had to be yanked harder until she made it to the top. A few feet behind, a little girl carried a fat chicken up the steps. A blur of feathers went swirling.

"What *is* this?" Paley asked, and as he spoke, a boy hurried by with two collies on leashes.

"It's the blessing of the animals," the boy called over his shoulder as he passed. "They do it every year at St. Christopher's."

Paley had always loved that idea. The cathedral was huge—huge enough to have a memorial service in a private chapel taking place at the same time as a blessing of the animals. He stood and watched the rest of the menagerie arrive. He saw two children walking ducks, a girl carrying a bowl of goldfish, an old man with a nervous-looking monkey perched on his shoulder. Maybe, Paley thought giddily, Larry Kelleher had been reincarnated as a primate. The air outside the church was suddenly filled with the smells and sounds of a zoo. A young girl emerged from the cathedral, crying out that anyone who saw her cat Lorenzo should let her know, but no one seemed to pay attention, so she bit her lip and went back inside. Paley wished he could say something to make her feel better, but just then Olive said to the group, "Come on. Enough with the Noah's ark business. Larry's service is about to begin."

So the Mental Midgets entered the cathedral single file, the same way they had entered Studio B every Tuesday night, so many years before. But instead of the wild applause that used to attend their arrival, now the air was filled with the mournful braying and yowling of animals.

The younger child of devout atheists, Jack Paley had been inside a house of worship only once in his life. And even then he had had to sneak in with his school friend Dennis McCarthy, because his own parents would have been outraged if they had known. It had been a Saturday afternoon, and the church had been empty except for a short, shuffling line outside the confessional. Paley had liked the easy comfort to be found in a church, the glossy, dark wood of the pews, the high rose windows, the lingering incense and intense silence. But Paley's interest wasn't exactly theological. When he thought back on that afternoon, what he remembered most vividly wasn't the atmosphere. It was, perversely, the mysterious red light above the confessional, blinking on when someone inside was resting on the kneeler, then off when the person had risen—a crude electrical triggering system that, for a ten-year-old with a scientific bent, was more compelling than the existence of God. For Paley, going to church was a huge sensory experience that he had gladly taken in all at once; he had sat in the church feeling like a dog being given its first car ride. Then he had gone home and told his parents that he'd been at Dennis's watching "Magilla Gorilla."

Now he settled into a pew in the back of the chapel. The crowd here was scattered, a disappointing turnout; but then, what could Paley have expected? After all, until the end of his life, Larry Kelleher had lived at home with his parents. He wasn't exactly out there in the world, being a bon vivant, going to nightclubs, taking tennis lessons, fending off throngs of women. The only speaker at the service, as it turned out, was the Professor.

"The loss of any life is, of course, tragic," the Professor began, standing behind the podium and smoothing down the crumpled pages of his speech. His voice caught, whether from emotion or stage fright, Paley couldn't tell; on the show, the Professor had never been the most effortless of hosts, but he'd managed to disguise the anxiety that gripped him—that gripped everyone back then—at showtime. Now he stared down at his prepared text, tracing the words with his finger. From beyond the glass door at the back of the chapel, somewhere in the cavernous reaches of the cathedral, two dogs barked. "The loss of a young life is, of course, even more profoundly tragic," the Professor continued. Great, Paley thought, a comparative study: tragic, more tragic—"Most tragic of all, however," the Professor went on, still not lifting his gaze, "is the waste of a mind. I was privileged to know Larry when his mind was at its sharpest, when his greatest gift of all was his potential. It seemed unlimited. Back then, it seemed as if Larry and his friends embodied nothing less than the future of America."

Paley shrank back against the bench. It was bad enough having to say farewell to his old friend Larry; did he really need to be reminded by his mentor of his *own* failings? As Paley looked around him, he noticed that both Tracy and Steve were wiping their eyes with the backs of their hands. And then Olive began to sniffle delicately. Soon Paley himself felt unspeakably sad. But he knew that none of the Mental Midgets, himself included, was really mourning their old friend, a colleague and competitor, Larry Kelleher. They were all mourning themselves. They were mourning the tragedy of their own lives: the young and the gifted, the very future of America, the prodigies who had done the unforgivable. *They'd grown up.*

And who could blame the Midgets for what they chose to mourn? Back then, the world had been both simple and stellar. Once a week they appeared on television, wedged between "The Bix Joplin Talk Show" and "Daddy Is a Warlock." Their place in the lineup was as fixed as their futures. And every week they *shone,* sometimes merely because everyone expected them to. When you know that millions of viewers are waiting for you to pull a stupendous answer out of thin air, then you *will* yourself to do so. Sometimes getting an answer right seemed to Paley an act of mental levitation: lifting up the deadweight that sat like a stone in the center of his mind in order to reveal the bed of glowing gems beneath. And what varied gems there were; although the Midgets answered questions in every category, each had a particular area of expertise. Paley's subject was Chemistry. Tracy's was Geography, Steve's was Word Derivations, Larry's was Classical Languages, Olive's was Astronomy, and Davy's was Physics. Together, they formed a formidable preteen think tank.

History had a way of turning all events into pleasant memories, and before Paley surrendered to nostalgia for the "Mental Midgets" he forced himself to remember the other side, the grueling study sessions, the infighting

among the group. The way homely, brilliant Dora Bunyan had been elbowed aside. The favoritism the producer clearly showed for pretty, aloof Olive Herne. The
petty jealousy that Paley could still feel for Olive at the
sight of her picture in a throwaway newspaper, let alone
on national TV. These were serious considerations, the
kinds of reservations that could—and probably did—keep
Paley awake nights. But, Paley also knew, Herzog had
been right: Those *were* the greatest years. Paley had
loved being a boy wonder—had loved it much more
than he sometimes was willing to admit. You weren't
supposed to peak at fourteen, he knew, yet he was afraid
that he had. And Studio B had been a wonderful place
to peak. For most kids, being brilliant was a liability, at
least socially. Girls didn't walk up to boys and say, "Is
that a slide rule in your pocket, or are you just happy to
see me?" But the Midgets could be brilliant and have
the world love them for it.

The show's producer, Tony Minion, a tall, leonine
man of forty, was especially impressed by the Midgets,
because he himself had not gone to college. "You kids
will inherit the earth," the handsome producer would
say every week when he wasn't too busy shouting at
them to work harder. Then he would disappear backstage to take a look at the set of questions that would be
asked on that night's show. The questions were written
by a panel of experts; only the Professor and Tony
Minion had access to them before showtime. Paley would
watch the two men walking around backstage minutes
before the telecast, and he would try to read their cryptic faces. *Am I going to embarrass myself out there?* he
would wonder, but neither man gave anything away.
And somehow, Paley would always succeed. He used
his intellect and his ambition to carry him through the
most difficult questions he'd ever heard. After he'd
answered correctly, the Professor would reward him

with the kindest, most beneficent of smiles; it was like the smile of God, and it made all the studying and worrying worthwhile.

It had been fifteen years since Paley saw that smile. He wasn't likely to see it today, he realized, here at a memorial service where the somber Professor was resolutely plowing through his speech. But then, Paley wasn't likely to ace any pop quizzes today, either. The kind of questions Paley found himself facing nowadays didn't lend themselves to the readily verifiable, right-or-wrong responses he'd had to produce during his cross-examination as a Mental Midget, or that Olive Herne still had to produce for her newspaper column. Paley's concerns these days, he realized, were more like essay questions to be answered in a blue book, or in the pages of *People:* "In twenty-five words or less, whatever happened to Jack Paley, the Mental Midget?"

In the distance, suddenly, a baby began to cry insistently—a plaintive, almost otherworldly sound. Its simple wail proved too much for the Professor, who suddenly curtailed his speech, thanked the congregation, and descended from the pulpit. It proved too much for Paley as well. There was nothing like the yowl of a baby to bring it all home, all the guilt, the loss, the regrets that accumulate over the years. The subject of babies was a particularly sensitive one for Paley, anyway; just recently Belinda had begun hinting at wanting to have a baby with him.

"You just want a baby, *generically,*" he'd responded. They were walking through Washington Square Park before work on the first morning of autumn. "You don't particularly want to have one with *me.*"

"Oh, sure," she said. "When I look at you, I see nothing more than a few million swimming sperm." She paused. "Come on, Paley, you know that isn't true. I think you'd be a great father for my baby."

"Your baby," he said. "That's just it. It would still be *yours,* Belinda, not ours. We're not at that fusion stage yet, you know, that stage where *we are one.* We don't have joint checking, and we only spend the night together once a week." He shook his head. "The baby can wait. And besides, do you think if we had a baby, we'd still have the freedom to go out for breakfast any morning we want?"

"Oh, Paley," she said, pulling at his arm. "Look around you."

He did. Everywhere Paley looked, he saw babies. He saw babies in strollers being pushed by speed-walking mothers. He saw babies in backpacks being carried by their awestruck fathers. He saw babies in perambulators, babies in arms, babies in bicycle baskets being wheeled around by parents no older than he. Where did all these babies come from? he wondered. Had they always been here, in this park along with all the homeless people and petty drug pushers and chess players? Were they a sight he'd selectively edited out of his line of vision? Or were they a new phenomenon, these babies with confident and capable parents, one of those fads that periodically infect the city, a trendy virus announced on the cover of *New York* magazine?

"You see, Paley?" Belinda said. "We're a whole new generation. We're the parents now."

"We aren't anything," Paley said, but maybe Belinda was right. Paley couldn't imagine his own parents starting the day by taking to the streets with their children; his parents belonged to the generation where the father disappeared to work first thing in the morning while the mother stayed home and drank and watched "The Days of Our Lives." And Belinda, a hardworking administrator at the TV station run by her father, didn't exactly seem a likely candidate for voluntary agoraphobia.

"Oh, come on, Paley," Belinda said. "Knock me up. You won't regret it."

"Knock you up?" he said, and he started to laugh. "Why, what an old romantic you are, Belinda." After that, the conversation was closed.

But sometimes, when Paley was alone and daydreaming, he imagined lying on the couch with Elvis Costello blaring out of the stereo speakers and a tiny baby clasped in his arms. But only sometimes. More often, he couldn't begin to imagine being somebody's father. He couldn't imagine hearing the word *Daddy* plaintively called out in a department store and having it refer to *him.* Before he could even begin to think about creating another life, he had to begin thinking about what to do with his own.

For a moment Paley wished that he was seven again and that the most burning question in his mind had to do with the atomic weight of zirconium. He wished that he was ten again and that he was still friends with Dennis McCarthy. The other Midgets must have been having similar thoughts of their own; when the service was over, they quickly filed out of the chapel in silence, and they might have dispersed without one more word, content not to see one another again until the next Mental Midget memorial service, if Steve hadn't suddenly spoken up when they'd reached the back of the church.

"Hey, Professor," he called out.

The Professor had scuttled ahead of the group, and he hesitated now with his back against the church door. He seemed trapped, caught in the act of making a secret getaway.

"Nice speech," Steve said, and the Professor relaxed. He smiled, and his eyes flooded. He stepped back inside the church and stood sniffling, his hands wringing the pages of his speech, while he accepted the tentative congratulations of all the Mental Midgets. But something was wrong with this picture. It was an uncharacteristic pose for the Professor; never before, Paley realized, had the Mental Midgets seen him looking vulnerable. He'd always been an invincible leader, gathering strength from his knowledge of how much they needed him. But now, with one of his charges suddenly gone, he seemed to be needing *them*.

It was an awkward moment, and Paley did what he often did on such occasions: He took advantage of his height to look over the heads of the people around him, into some indefinite middle distance where he was guaranteed not to have to make eye contact.

Where his gaze settled now was a corner of the church where a confessional waited, red lights blazing above both doors. A couple of people were standing in line, and Paley fleetingly thought about joining them. His lack of religious training never bothered Paley, but in some weird way he longed to be kneeling now in the dark, unloading his guilt. Just then one of the red lights blinked off. *A sign!* Paley thought. But then it blinked on again before anyone emerged, and Paley figured it was just as well. What would he have said to the priest? In a catalogue of personal failings, where could he have possibly begun? *Let's see. I haven't been living up to my fullest potential. The most profound tragedy is the waste of a human mind, and I've wasted mine on alcohol. I flirt, I smoke too much, and I think I used to be a whole lot smarter. Also, I once lied to my parents about watching "Magilla Gorilla."*

The red light blinked off again. This time Paley strode over to the confessional.

"Paley. Hey, Jack," Tracy called to him, but he didn't turn around. Instead, he just kept walking, past the line outside the confessional, past the door where the red light was lit, to the other door, where the red light was dark. Paley waited a moment. It blinked back on. He knocked on the door. When nobody answered, he pulled it open.

The Extra Credit Question is:

What Did Paley Expect to Find?

(Solution on next page)

∫olution

Paley bent down in the doorway so that he would block the exit of a small white cat. He scooped the cat up into his arms and turned around, facing the rows of pews. "Are you Lorenzo?" he asked loudly, his voice resonant in the cathedral. Sure enough, a small girl came running down the aisle—this time beaming.

"Lorenzo!" she shrieked, and Paley delivered the cat to its owner.

"Showing off, Paley?" Olive said when he rejoined the Midgets.

He shrugged. "I just couldn't get the sound of the crying baby during the Professor's eulogy out of my head. Then when I saw the blinking red light above the confessional, I put it all together. How many times have we all heard a yowling cat in the middle of the night that sounds just like a yowling baby? Well, I guessed that Lorenzo had slipped into the confessional and couldn't get out, and he was making the light blink by stepping *on and off the kneeler.*"

"You should be a dog and cat catcher!" said the little girl, looking up from the cat cradled in her arms.

A couple of the Midgets smirked, but Paley drew himself tall and straight.

"Please," he corrected. "Dog and cat *consultant.*"

Chapter Three
THE YEAR
OF THE CHAMELEON

At half past eleven on a cool evening in October, when taxis bumped slowly over nearly empty avenues, when the last stragglers walked home from Korean markets, tired arms balancing bags of groceries, when the roar of the city seemed to be lowered several notches, Paley and Belinda were revving themselves up for the start of another Tuesday night at the movies. They had just finished making love, and they found themselves replenished and possessed of an almost superhuman energy. Outside, the city was starting to slumber, but in Belinda's apartment, every light was blazing and the night was young.

"I'm so psyched," said Paley, popping a videotape out of a black plastic box. Earlier that evening he'd biked to the Montevideo Video Store, a common stop on his Tuesday night rounds, and carefully selected a tape. Now, sitting on Belinda's huge bed with a punch bowl full of hot popcorn in front of them, Paley leaned forward and slid the tape into the machine. It swallowed the tape obediently; in a moment the screen was filled with the familiar, comically stern warning from the FBI—a sorry substitute for a curtain parting in a real theater, but it would have to do. Paley leaned back against the giant floral pillows with Belinda curled companionably against him. She smelled of shampoo and butter, and Paley almost reflexively buried his head into her neck. But this wasn't the time to start anything. *This* was showtime.

"And that concludes our coming attractions," he'd said to Belinda a few minutes ago, rolling over in bed to snap on a reading lamp.

"We're in big trouble," she'd answered, "if you think the movie is the main event."

He'd laughed lightly with her, but in a way it was true: The movies were a semiregular ritual, an illicit pleasure. The time felt stolen; long after the rest of the city had turned out its lights, Belinda and Paley would still be coaxing extra hours out of the day. Paley usually dawdled in the unbearable fluorescence of the video store, trying to find a movie to match his mood, but in the end the selection almost didn't matter. The movie wouldn't disappoint, couldn't fail to meet his or Belinda's anticipation of that moment when they settled down together in front of the flickering image of the RKO radio tower or the Columbia goddess or the Warner Brothers shield.

Today Fly-By-Night had assigned Paley to a fashion shoot in Central Park. He had spent the morning adjusting arc lights and routing pedestrians out of camera range, but after lunch the photographer, a brooding figure of indeterminate gender in a black turtleneck, had instructed him to don a woolen winter coat and scarf, mingle among the cluster of male models behind a woman in tartan plaid, and throw back his head as if he'd just heard a joke. Paley didn't have to act; this was a blast. He got to pass an afternoon under a brilliant autumn sky, his elegant attire color-coordinated with the ambers and russets of the trees, his jaw dropped open in honest hilarity. And he'd been well rewarded; he'd made more money in four hours as a model than in his previous four weeks as a temp. He'd even been flattered; when the photographer's assistant saw his reaction to the paycheck, she'd shaded her eyes, squinted up at Paley, and said, "Handsome pay for handsome work." He'd barely noticed her, however; Paley was thinking about the night ahead.

The weeks rose and fell around his Tuesdays with Belinda now. He was reminded of his childhood, and the graceful arc the weeks described then, the heightening excitement leading up to, then the pleasant exhaustion leading away from, the night of the "Mental Midgets" broadcast. He suspected that he'd chosen Tuesday as his night with Belinda in some kind of subconscious homage to the Tuesday nights of old. In some ways his life hadn't changed in all those years; by the time Tuesday evening came around nowadays, Paley might as well have been twelve again.

"Within one mile," Mrs. Cellini had called after him in the hall tonight, "what's the ground distance between New York City and Chicago?"

"Eight hundred and one," Paley answered over his shoulder.

"Eight hundred and two!" he heard from behind as he unlocked his door. "Correct!"

Inside his apartment the answering machine was blinking. He rewound the tape and listened as Davy Herzog, with his old mysterioso approach, suggested it might be in Paley's best interest to call him back. But Paley had no time to make the call, or even to wonder what was on Herzog's mind. It was getting late, and he wanted to get to the video store before all the good tapes were gone and the only choices left were *Bobby Deerfield* or *The Shoes of the Fisherman*. Paley made quick work of the obligatory bath and shave. He flipped on the TV for company while he pulled on a pair of black button-fly jeans that Belinda particularly favored; as soon as he'd answered Final Jeopardy ("What is the great vowel shift?" he said, and he was out the door), he biked the four blocks over to Montevideo's.

Here, in front of the "Classics" rack, Paley caught his breath. The empty boxes with tiny artwork could actually make him feel light-headed, like a child surrounded by too many birthday presents. It was too good to be true, having the entire history of Hollywood only an arm's length away, and Paley often wouldn't know where to plunge in. But tonight he did: *The Philadelphia Story*. No, he couldn't have made a better choice for the evening, he thought later. It was breezy, sophisticated, sexy—not unlike Belinda. In certain ways, Belinda reminded him of the Katharine Hepburn character in the movie. Tracy Lord and Belinda Frank were both blue of blood and long of leg.

"You know why I love renting movies that were made before the 1950s?" Paley said, pulling the popcorn bowl closer.

"Because the aspect ratio for movies back then was approximately the same height and width as a TV screen's is now, so none of the image is lost, as it is with movies photographed in a wide-screen process," Belinda said.

"I've told you that before."

"You tell me that every time we watch a movie, Paley."

"Oh."

He grabbed a handful of popcorn and watched as the first credit faded in: the MGM lion.

"This is it," Paley whispered.

But somehow, this wasn't it. Something was different. Paley squinted, momentarily disoriented. "I got the wrong movie," he said weakly, staring at the Technicolor image on the screen. "This movie's supposed to be B and W, Lindy."

"What?" she asked distractedly. "Shh, baby, I'm watching."

The title card appeared, and the words *The Philadelphia Story* flashed boldly across the screen . . . in *green.* Paley scrambled to his knees, almost knocking over the popcorn bowl.

"What's going on here?" he said. "This is sacrilege! That movie's a black-and-white classic. Who tampered with it?"

"Honey," Belinda began, but Paley wasn't listening. "Honey, I have to tell you something."

"This is *terrible,*" he interrupted. "How can they take a terrific movie like that and wantonly add color to it? Next thing you know, Katharine Hepburn's hair will be red or something!"

"It *is* red," Belinda murmured.

"That's not the point," said Paley. He swung his legs over the side of the bed and sat with his head in his hands. "Her hair is supposed to be black-and-white. Everything is. I guess I'll have to report this to STANDARDS."

"To what?"

"It's an organization," said Paley. "The letters stand for Stopping the Arbitrary Negating, Doctoring, and Retouching of Directorial . . . Standards."

"You're making this up."

"I know how it sounds," Paley said. "We're kind of a fringe group, I admit, but that's what purists are."

"*We?*"

"I only sent them ten bucks," Paley said sheepishly. "Real members are more committed. They're the ones who mount guerrilla attacks."

"I see," said Belinda.

"I can't," said Paley. He turned toward the screen,

staring one more time at the offending array of colors: the nauseatingly green wallpaper, the preposterously matching fuschia of the suit and hat worn by Jimmy Stewart, the salmon skin tone of Katharine Hepburn that nature would never impose on a human face. "I can't watch," he said. "Let's get out of here."

"Don't be a drag," said Belinda. "It's almost midnight."

"It's *Mister* Drag to you," Paley said. "Besides, since when do we ever get to sleep early on a Tuesday night?"

"But where in the world are we going to go?" Then she paused. "Oh, don't tell me," she said. "I should have guessed."

Paley nodded. "It's the only thing that will cheer me up," he said.

"We could turn the color down on the TV," Belinda offered. "It'll look just like black and white then," she went on, but already Paley had bounded off the bed, retrieving his black jeans from the radiator where they'd landed earlier in the evening. Belinda sighed dramatically, and then she, too, began to dress. Paley watched the curve of her spine as she bent to pull on first a cream-colored slip, then her black silk blouse and skirt. It was midnight, but she looked terrific. She looked as good as Katharine Hepburn might have looked, if only those movie vandals had left her alone.

Fung's All-Night Noodle Parlor was located down a bright arcade, an island of light in the middle of a dark block in the heart of Chinatown. Even though it was so late, crowds still milled along the lit walkway. People gathered around a chicken that played tic-tac-toe for quarters. Eerie, high-pitched music, which Paley discerned to be the Chinese rendition of "Stairway to Heaven," wafted from the doorway of a store that featured Bruce Lee memorabilia. But at the end of the arcade, its windows steamed over with the promise of hot food inside, Fung's waited. If Paley couldn't escape to screwball Main Line Philadelphia, at least he could lose himself in a tureen of noodles and tree-ear mushrooms in broth.

"We have a good table for you and your lady friend!" Fung himself said as Paley and Belinda waited at the cash register. Paley had stumbled across this place while serving his jury duty at the criminal courts building a couple of blocks away; hardly a week passed that he didn't pay a return visit. Fung led the couple across the room, to the table beneath a huge mural of Chairman and Madame Mao waving to a flock of workers. The painting was frighteningly realistic, right down to the proliferation of moles.

Paley watched as a fleet of waiters rushed by carrying pots of aromatic noodles. He inhaled. In a few minutes, after he'd drunk several thimbles of dark, flowery tea, he began to relax.

"What year were you born?" Belinda asked.

"You know that," said Paley. But he realized that she was staring down at her place mat, and he glanced down at his, too, then said, "The year of the monkey."

"I'm the year of the snake," said Belinda.

Paley pounded his fist on the still-damp table. "Dammit, woman, then we can't be together; it would be miscegenation. Our children would exist on a diet of . . . bananas and field mice!"

Belinda smiled. "You seem in better spirits," she said.

"Sort of," he admitted. "But I can't stop thinking about the movie."

In a moment the waiter brought their order over, and Paley hunkered down above his bowl and sucked up a few long strands. From across the table, he could see Belinda watching him.

"Eat," he grunted.

"I'm not hungry," she said. She kept watching him. "Paley," she finally said, and something in her tone made him look up warily. "You shouldn't let these things get to you. They're just not worth it."

"They *are* worth it," he said. "They're exactly what makes the world go round." He heard himself, and he sounded foolish—or worse, naive. "Look," he went on, absently rooting through the noodles with his chopsticks, "I know it doesn't compare with being Albert Schweitzer or finding a cure for AIDS, but sometimes something as simple as the purity of a black-and-white movie at the end of a day *can* make a difference. The thing is, Belinda, you don't know how much I've been looking forward to this evening."

"Me, too," she said softly. Then she took a deep breath. "Paley, back at the apartment I tried to tell you something, but you cut me off."

Paley raised an eyebrow. "Belinda, if this is one of those conversations where the woman tells the man she loves him like a brother more than a lover, this *isn't* the time for it."

"Paley," she said. "It's about colorization."

He paused. "Colorization?"

"Yeah," she said. "I know a little bit about the subject myself. You see, at work, my father has been talking nonstop about it. It's his latest obsession. I've been reading all the literature on it that I can find. He's thinking seriously about hiring someone at the station to make decisions about all the old movies in the film library. He's holding interviews for the position tomorrow morning."

Paley delicately crossed his chopsticks on his plate. "Belinda," he said softly. "How can you sit back and let it happen?"

"I'm uneasy about it," she said. "I've talked it over with my father, but he seems set in his ways. You know how he is."

Paley nodded. Although Paley and Stewart Frank had met only three or four times, there was a distinct uneasiness between them—the special brand of uneasiness that often occurs between fathers and the men who are sleeping with their daughters. Both of them tried to ignore it, to work around it, and to be relaxed in each other's presence, but it was an elaborate and not very convincing charade. Every time they met, Belinda's father squeezed Paley's hand in his own ham-sized hand. Stewart Frank often expressed interest in Paley's work, but Paley noticed that Stewart never once made eye contact with him. He always seemed to be making *eyebrow* contact, or *nostril* contact. It all made Paley quite nervous. Belinda's father wasn't a bad man, personally; he was just a big, blustery, uncomfortable man with inconsistent values. Paley would occasionally read that Stewart had donated a large sum of money to a worthy cause—a shelter for battered women, a day-care center, a hurricane relief fund—but of course Stewart was also quite vocal about his belief that Nixon had gotten a bum deal. It didn't add up. The thing was, the guy was *nice*. Well meaning, evasive, rich. He favored candy-striped shirts with white collars, and red ties held in place by little gold safety pins. He always looked unselfconsciously pleased as punch to be rich. But Paley couldn't discuss any of this with Belinda; the matter was further complicated by the fact that Belinda worked for her father, as a programmer at the network. Belinda adored her father, and he was absolutely crazy about her. When she was a little girl, she had told Paley, her father would come to every one of her events at the Crumley School: every band concert, every play, every gymnastics competition. Most of the other fathers were equally busy and wealthy, but only Stewart had a perfect attendance record. And he always sat in the first row, grinning and waving at his daughter.

Now Paley wiped soy sauce from his mouth and said hesitantly, "I'd love to ask your father how he can advocate that kind of thing."

"So," Belinda said, "ask him."

"Right."

"I mean it," she said, and at long last she picked up er chopsticks. "I care about films as much as you do, Paley. But I'm tired, I'm hungry, I have to get up for work in the morning, and I'm sick of talking about this. Let's give this subject a rest for the night, and then in the morning you can come down to the station and ask my father yourself. Stop by at nine, and maybe you can talk to him before the interviews start at ten."

"You forget," said Paley. "I'm gainfully employed."

"You also made a bundle today as a fashion stud," she said. "You can afford to take a morning off. This is your big chance, Paley. You're the one who's always saying how you'd like to change the world."

"I am?"

"You're the one who gave money to STANDARDS. You're the one who's always telling me that my position in the corporate infrastructure carries with it certain responsibilities to society. You're the one who's always saying I should try to use my influence to effect change from within the system."

"I'm the one who's always telling you to bring back reruns of 'The Mary Tyler Moore Show,' " Paley tried.

"Listen," she said, moving aside a teapot to get a better view of him. "Do you want to talk to my father or not?"

Paley thought about meeting with Stewart Frank first thing in the morning; he thought about what it would be like starting his day with a Masculine Handshake Competition. But then he thought about Katharine Hepburn's high cheekbones, and their bizarre salmon-colored glow.

"All right," said Paley. "I'll be there."

*   *   *

"So, Jack," Stewart Frank began, pumping Paley's hand before pointing him to a deep leather chair. "Always a pleasure to see you around the office. What can I do you for?"

"Actually, Stewart," Paley said, "I'm here to get an education."

"An education?" Belinda's father stroked his face, as though checking his morning shave.

"It was my idea," said Belinda. "I thought Paley could benefit from hearing some experts make the case for colorization."

"Colorization," said her father, leaning back in his chair, the sun streaming down on him from his wall of windows. "Who needs to make a case for it? Colorization perks up dreary old movies. Makes everything a little bit cheerier. What with the day-to-day problems of the average man, why not come home at night to a vision of a kinder, gentler, more *colorful* world?" He turned expectantly to Paley and Belinda.

"Colorful?" Paley said. "Why don't you colorize Ingmar Bergman movies, too, while you're at it? It's too depressing, all that Swedish melodrama. Let's colorize *The Seventh Seal!* I want to see a red-and-black chess board, the way God wanted it!" His voice was infused with anger.

Stewart leaned forward. "I thought you wanted an education," he said quietly. "It sounds to me like you've got your mind made up already."

"Sorry," said Paley. Belinda squeezed his arm. He could feel her declawed fingers pressing lightly into his skin. "I do want to learn more about it," Paley said. "I guess I got a little carried away."

"All right then," said Stewart. "If you really want to learn, this is the place. We have state-of-the-art equipment here." He chuckled. "We've even got a colorization lab that I've nicknamed The Rainbow Room. Pretty clever, no?"

"Clever," Paley admitted weakly.

"Well," said Stewart, "Jack here can sit in on the interviews if he doesn't act up. No more sarcastic comments about Ingrid Bergman. She was a lovely actress, even if she did have that baby out of wedlock."

"Ingmar," Paley corrected, but Stewart was already onto the next order of business, calling into his intercom that his secretary should send the first colorization candidate in.

The man's name was Fred Entwhistle, and he was as pale as flour. He spoke eloquently and forcefully of the need for old films to find new audiences. He admitted to having some reservations about the colorization process, but he acknowledged that radical steps might be necessary to make classic films palatable for contemporary audiences. He also argued that such procedures need not compromise the integrity of the filmmaker, and he asserted that he would attempt, to the best of his abilities, to remain faithful to the original cinematic vision. Entwhistle reminded Paley of the nearsighted, middle-aged men he sometimes saw at the afternoon screenings in the Museum of Modern Art, sitting alone in the auditorium, squinting at their film notes, poking their glasses back up their noses.

"Hmm," is all Stewart said when Fred Entwhistle had thanked them all for their time and excused himself from the room. Paley didn't take this as a good sign. "Well," Stewart added after a few moments, "perhaps we should see what the next candidate has to offer."

The next applicant was Stanley Waxman, a name that Paley vaguely recalled. It wasn't until Waxman referred to his time in Hollywood that Paley put it together.

"I'm sorry to interrupt," Paley said, "but if you're *the* Stanley Waxman, then I'm certainly familiar with your work."

Waxman looked uneasily pleased. "Well, thanks," he

said. "It's nice to know that there are actually *viewers* out there. I'm not exactly Steven Spielberg."

Stewart Frank looked puzzled, and Belinda leaned over and said, "Mr. Waxman is a director."

"Was," corrected Waxman. "And I only made one movie."

"Maybe I've seen it," said Stewart, consulting Waxman's résumé.

"Actually," said Waxman, "you own it. It was one of the movies you acquired in the Monumental Pictures takeover."

"Cheerleader Chainsaw Massacre?" Stewart read from the résumé. "I think I missed that one."

"Well, I'm not surprised," said Waxman. "Most people did. I never liked those kinds of movies myself, but when the offer came along, I figured a job's a job."

"Amen," said Stewart.

"The only problem is," Waxman went on, "I never had the stomach for it. Half the people who went to my movie got mad because it wasn't gory enough. And the other half got mad because it had too much blood. And then somebody at *Sight & Sound* got the bright idea I was making a political statement about slasher movies. That's probably why *you* saw it," he said to Paley.

Paley admitted that it was.

"I'm not saying I didn't put a lot of thought and effort into the film," said Waxman, "but believe me, there's nothing that can kill a career faster in Hollywood than an arty, experimental reputation. I guess what I'm saying is that I think my experience qualifies me for this job here. I can understand why some people would hate the idea of movies being tampered with."

Stewart shifted in his chair.

"But I can understand why other people would want to see them in color."

Paley shifted in his chair.

"Either way," said Waxman, "it's show biz. Am I right?"

When he'd left the room, both Stewart and Paley had to admit that he had a point.

"Well, he seems like the perfect compromise candidate," said Belinda. "He's straightforward and he's realistic, and he has a conscience."

"Yes, Lindy," said her father, "but with all due respect to Jack here, I'm not interested in a compromise candidate. I don't want someone working for me who's only going to do half the job."

"Of course," said Belinda. "We do have one more applicant to interview. His name is Carl Thorn, and he comes highly recommended."

The secretary brought him in. Carl Thorn was a young man with a ready laugh and a bow tie and the ability to look you right in the eye. Paley didn't trust him one bit. Neither, Paley saw, did Stewart. As soon as Thorn started unreeling his spiel, Stewart leaned forward in his chair, his brows bent, his chin puckering.

"The way I see it," Thorn began, "is like this. Some people say colorization is a way to get today's audiences to watch old movies. Some people say colorization is a crime against art. But you know what I say?"

He paused dramatically, swiveling his head until he'd made eye contact with every person in the room.

"I say colorization is good business."

Stewart's eyebrows unbowed.

"And you know why it's good business?" Carl Thorn continued. "Because it's what people want. I colorized *Psycho,* and people *loved* knowing that the blood going down the drain is red. I colorized *The African Queen,* and people *loved* knowing that Katharine Hepburn's hair is blond."

"I thought her hair is red," Paley interrupted.

"It is," said Thorn, "but when I was done with it, it

was blond and people *loved* it. All I'm saying is why not give people what they want? Because if you don't, somebody else will. Somebody else will put these movies into color. Somebody else will make the money that's waiting to be made. And that, my friends, is just plain bad business."

"Amen," Stewart said, glancing meaningfully at Paley.

Paley cleared his throat. "What about STANDARDS?" he said.

"That bunch of radicals?" said Thorn. "Long after they realize they're fighting a losing battle, people are going to be watching colorized movies. And every time they do, Mr. Frank," he said, lowering his voice and turning back toward Stewart, "I want to make sure you get your piece of the action."

"Call me Stewart," he said. "But what's all this about radicals?"

"Never mind," said Paley. "It's not important." He loosened his tie, swallowed, then said, "Stewart, I think we've probably heard all we need to hear for the morning. If you'll allow me to put my two cents in, I think you should go ahead and hire Mr. Thorn."

"Mr. *Thorn!*" said Stewart and Belinda in unison.

"That's my name," said the candidate, smiling anxiously. "Don't wear it out, ha ha."

"I simply think Mr. Thorn is the right choice," Paley continued evenly.

"Well," said Stewart, "I must say I have no objection to hiring Mr. Thorn. Belinda?"

"You said I might be useful in helping you reach a decision," said Paley, and he reached for Belinda's hand.

Belinda looked from her father to Paley and then back to her father. And then Paley squeezed her hand, reminding her that, in the end, he was on *her* side.

"I did say that," she said. "I guess I have no objection, either. Mr. Thorn, we'll discuss specifics later in the week, if that's all right.''

"Fine, fine,'' said Thorn. He shook hands all around, looked everybody in the eye, and then was directed by Stewart's secretary upstairs to personnel.

"Paley,'' Stewart said when the door closed, "I must say, you surprise me.''

"I'll say,'' said Belinda.

"Well, I said I wanted to hear somebody make the case for colorization. And Mr. Thorn certainly did that.''

"So this has turned out to be an educational experience for you after all,'' said Stewart with obvious satisfaction.

"Yes, it has,'' said Paley. He ran his hand over the face of his watch. "And now, if you don't mind, your daughter and I have a lunch date.''

"We do?''

"Go!'' said Stewart. "Eat well. You've certainly earned your keep around here today.'' As Paley and Belinda left the office, they could hear her father humming a Johnny Mathis song.

Belinda waited until she and Paley were outside the building before she looked at him, squinting in the open sunlight.

"Okay,'' she said, "now suppose you tell me what that was all about.''

"Maybe I just got carried away with my introduction to high-level executive decision-making,'' he said.

"And?''

"Okay,'' Paley said, "I'll be glad to tell you,'' and he waved for a taxi. A cab cut across three lanes of traffic and pulled to the curb. "But only if you go somewhere with me.''

"What?'' she said. "Where?''

"To the movies.''

"I'd love to. But I have work to do.''

"Come on, Lindy. It'll be the date we never had last night. Didn't you say that all week you'd been looking forward to our Tuesday evening together?"

"Yes," she said. "But now we're talking about Wednesday afternoon."

"We're also talking about *The Philadelphia Story*," he said, climbing into the backseat. "It's showing at the Biograph."

Belinda didn't answer. She stood on the sidewalk, her arms folded, her face tilted in a mixture of curiosity and exasperation.

"I'm not going anywhere until you tell me what happened back in my father's office," she said.

"Okay," he said, "hop in."

The Extra Credit Question is:

What Did Paley Tell Her?

(Solution on next page)

∫olution

As the cab bounced uptown, Paley said, "First, Carl Thorn is an impostor."

"What?" said Belinda. "What do you mean? And why didn't you tell me? If that's the case, we shouldn't be hiring him."

"Sure you should," Paley said, "if you care about the future of film."

"I'm afraid you've lost me."

"Well, he knew what STANDARDS was."

"But that doesn't prove anything," she said. "Okay, maybe *I* didn't know about the organization. But Paley, this is someone who's worked in colorization. It makes sense he would know about it."

"Not the way I phrased it to him. What about STAN-DARDS?' doesn't necessarily refer to a radical organization."

"But still—"

"I know, I know," Paley said. "It still doesn't prove anything. But I only mentioned the organization because I already suspected he was an impostor. He said he'd worked in colorization."

"Right."

"And he said that among the films he'd worked on were *Psycho* and *The African Queen.*"

"Right."

"Only *The African Queen* was *originally made in color.*"

"It was?"

"I'm sure of it. I remember how surprised I was when I saw it in a theater the first time. You know, you see Bogart, you naturally think black and white."

"But still—"

"I know, I know," said Paley. "Why hire him? Well, you'd be the first to agree there's no stopping your father once he makes up his mind."

"I suppose," she said.

"Well, I suspect that Thorn is a member of STAN-DARDS. You won't try to stop him, will you?"

"Stop him from *what?*" she said, regarding Paley uneasily.

"Whatever. If STANDARDS *is* involved, it might be fun to see what they have in mind for your father. It won't be anything dangerous. And who knows—it just might provide *him* with an education."

Belinda shook her head and turned away. As she looked out the window, she continued shaking her head, as if she were watching a tennis match. And, Paley thought, she was—between her father and her boyfriend.

"Well," she said after a long silence, "I guess now we'll know just how much change can be effected by one person working within the system."

At the theater, they bought a bucket of popcorn, and they settled into their seats just as the auditorium was darkening. Paley leaned back; Belinda curled against him. The curtains parted, and the MGM lion roared to life on the screen, in glorious black and white.

"I'm so psyched," Belinda said.

Chapter Four
THE RIDDLER

I'VE got one for you."

Paley hadn't heard these words in a very long time, and now they caused a chill of memory to slide along his arms. It had been fifteen years since he and Herzog had played the riddle game. What had started out as a way to pass time in the green room at the studio had turned into an obsession.

The riddles in the game were a far cry from "What does it mean when your clock strikes thirteen?" These were *complex* riddles, and when Paley was a Mental Midget, he couldn't wait for the moment during the day when Herzog would give him a sidelong glance and utter those five familiar words. It was like having a friend on the front stoop, calling into the intercom, "Mrs. Paley, can Jack come out and play?"

Now, fifteen years later, Paley was no less delighted by the invitation. It was astonishing how quickly a person could revert to an earlier self, an earlier obsession, he thought as he struggled to pull off his jacket while cradling the telephone against his shoulder. The phone had started ringing the moment Paley walked in the door. He owned one of those cheapo Brand X telephones with a ring that sounds like locusts in heat; because the sound was so painful he always rushed to answer the phone on its first ring.

After he heard Herzog's voice and accustomed himself to the sudden wave of nostalgia, Paley sank back into his big armchair by the window. It had been an especially long but enjoyable day. Fly-By-Night had sent him off to the Museum of Modern Art to extemporize on Abstract Expressionism to third-graders. ("Can *you* say Willem de Kooning, boys and girls?") When Paley was about to leave for the day, he got lost in the middle of a swell of people entering the museum for an evening cocktail party in honor of some young new painter. The painter, it turned out, was Zack Taplinger, a friend of Paley's from boarding school. Zack had been famous for being the campus cartoonist; every week he would draw caricatures of students and teachers for the school newspaper. For a while the two boys were so close that they had been known as Jack 'n' Zack, but after prep school they gradually lost touch. Zack went out to California to paint; Paley often heard that he had gone on to great success. Just how great wasn't apparent to him until now, when he saw his old friend striding into the museum to the accompanying pop of flashbulbs.

"Zack!" he called.

"Jack!" his friend called back.

Zack Taplinger wore a black tuxedo with a candy-striped cummerbund. His long hair was the same length it had been in tenth grade, except now it was threaded through with premature silver. After Paley and Zack had hugged and joked about the impossibility of recapping the past thirteen years, a wily art dealer managed to yank Zack off into a corner to meet some investors from Texas, and Paley found himself in the middle of a room full of people and huge canvases of "Archie" characters in pornographic poses. He mingled, he wor-

ried about being underdressed, he squinted at Betty and
Veronica curled together in the backseat of Archie's
jalopy, he ate canapés that looked like miniature Christ-
mas presents until his stomach was pleasantly full and
he was ready to go. By the time he checked his watch,
it was already nine o'clock.

Now, sitting at home, Paley loosened his tie, opened
his shirt at the collar, and shut off the overhead light.
Playing the riddle game with Herzog was a perfect, if
unexpected, way to end the day. In the distance a car
alarm whooped mournfully, but he didn't mind. "I'm
ready," he said. "Probably a little rusty, but ready."

"A man," Herzog began, "invites a friend to have a
drink, but tells him he has to wear a suit."

"That's *it?*"

"That's it."

Paley pretended to be outraged by the dearth of information, but this, too, was part of the game. The riddles
were supposed to be as spare as haiku. He remembered
the first one Herzog had ever tried on him: "John and
Mary are lying naked and dead in the living room,
surrounded by water and broken glass." That was it.

It had been up to Paley to pepper Herzog with questions that could be answered yes or no, breaking down
the ambiguities of the situation one by one until at last
he had divined the singular set of circumstances leading
up to it: John and Mary were *goldfish;* the water and
glass came from their fishbowl, which the cat had knocked
over.

The second time they played the game, Herzog had
begun with, "A man gets in his car and drives to work,
but halfway there he turns around, goes home, and kills
his wife." That was it. Paley had asked a battery of
questions and had gotten a few more clues from them,
but he couldn't make the whole thing work, and he'd
left the green room stumped. Two days later, in the

middle of the night, the solution simply appeared: The man had been listening to the radio while driving to work, and the show had been the kind in which the announcer picks a name at random, calls that person at home, and if the party answers, informs him he has won a cash prize. That day, the announcer had called the man's home, where his wife was supposedly alone, but the person who answered the phone was *another man.* The wife was having an affair, so the husband turned around, went home, and shot her.

Another time Herzog had begun, "A man gets in an elevator and presses the button for the tenth floor, but before he reaches the seventh floor he knows his wife has died."

This one had been Paley's favorite. First he had to confirm not only that the man was going to the tenth floor because he lived there, but also that his wife was, indeed, home—since nothing in this game could ever be taken for granted. Next Paley had to figure out that the elevator had stalled due to a power failure—a key piece of information that Herzog had conveniently omitted from his narrative. Finally Paley had to make the leap from the power failure to the death of the wife: she had been hooked up to an *iron lung.*

"A man invites a friend over but tells him he has to wear a suit," Paley repeated now. "Sounds intriguing. God, can you believe how long it's been since we played this game?"

"This time," Herzog said, "it's not just a game."

"What do you mean?"

Herzog sighed. "I mean the invitation is real," he said. "Suit and all. I've got to see you. Tonight. Now."

"Look, I've been out all day," Paley tried, "and I'm really beat. I've been so busy lately, and it's getting to me, Herzog."

"Ah, *busy,* the great Manhattan affliction," said

Herzog. "If you want to meet up with someone in this city, you have to make plans prenatally. What have you been busy with, Paley—racquetball? Lunch at the Harvard Club?"

"My life," said Paley simply.

"It's okay," said Davy. "I *do* know you're busy, what with all that temp work. I don't mean to whine, but I really need to see you. Soon."

The urgency in his voice came as a surprise. The Mental Midgets had never expressed real need to one another. When you were a genius, you were supposed to get along fine in the world without asking for help. Real geniuses, Paley had read in the paper, rarely went into therapy. Real geniuses didn't need shoulders to cry on, they needed blackboards to write on. When you were a genius, your own presence was supposed to be enough to carry you through life. You could figure out problems on your own, amuse yourself on the subway by mumbling aloud Plato's "Parable of the Cave." So what if the people sitting next to you inched away? The important thing was that the shadows on the walls of your mind would flicker forever, and never die.

This certainly wasn't true of Paley, and apparently it wasn't true of Davy Herzog either. Paley felt a sudden wave of empathy for twisted little Herzog. He was reminded of being at Harvard and in despair, propped up on his narrow bed overlooking the Yard, sipping slowly at a bottle of gin as the hours melted, watching healthy young men and women walk with books under their arms, watching the stone pillars of the Widener Library start to glaze over in the drunken afternoon light. Maybe Herzog was in despair now, too. Maybe it had to do with drinking, maybe with love, maybe with being almost thirty and lost. Whatever it was, maybe Paley could offer a little compassion.

But it wasn't only compassion that Paley felt as he

listened to Herzog's constrained voice and labored breathing, and it wasn't only an act of charity that made Paley stay on the line. It was more than that. He was like Herzog, he was *part of* Herzog. For years Paley had barely thought about any of the Mental Midgets, except in dreams, when the whole group of them appeared in their miniature caps and gowns like a flock of baby blackbirds. Now Herzog was asking Paley to meet him that night for a drink, and Paley was agreeing as if in a trance. His words were robotic; he didn't understand where they had come from. He didn't really *like* Davy Herzog, and he certainly wasn't going to have a "drink" with him, at least not anything alcoholic. But he knew that he was drawn to Herzog the way people are drawn to their families. Year after year, adult children trudge home to spend Thanksgiving with bitter, squabbling families in an overheated apartment, and although nobody really gets along and someone is bound to burst into tears before the meal is through, they fit around the table perfectly. Paley somehow fit in with Davy. He fit in with all the Midgets, for that matter, more than he fit in anywhere. He was actually glad that Herzog had called.

"Meet me at eleven-thirty, if it's not too late," said Herzog. He gave the address of O'Shea's, a bar-restaurant on lower Madison Avenue.

"Can't you take a subway down here?" Paley asked.

"No!" Herzog said. "It wouldn't be the same. And don't forget," he added. "Wear a suit."

"A suit. You were serious. Okay, I'll bite. Why?"

"That," Herzog said, "is the game."

Then he hung up, leaving Paley wondering what he had just agreed to.

At least Paley didn't have to change his clothes; he was still wearing the suit in which he had gone to work that morning. It was an Italian cut, pure linen the color of caramel, and it made him look "drop-dead gorgeous," or so he'd been told by Lynn, the paralegal who'd given it to him for his birthday two years before. Belinda didn't appreciate the personal history that came with the suit, so Paley didn't get many chances to wear it. But when one *did* come along, when he was specifically requested to dress for an occasion as he had been this morning by the agency, and as he had been now—*that,* Paley told himself as he left the apartment, was too good to pass up.

But why a suit? Maybe, Paley thought as the cab he had hailed traveled across Fourteenth Street, the answer had to do with the dress code at O'Shea's. But that seemed too obvious, and this game was anything but. O'Shea's turned out to be located on one of those stretches of Madison Avenue where the office buildings all seem to be the kind that house countless corridors leading to numberless cubicles. The coffee shops downstairs do their best business at breakfast, the health-food salad bars cater to a secretary's diet and budget at lunch, and the restaurants with the awnings out front thrive on executives' expense accounts. Some of these restaurants keep their bars open into the early evening hours, picking up a few extra dollars from the occasional midlevel types desperate for a hideaway to carry out a tryst. The later these places stay open, the more desperate the customers. And as far as Paley could tell, O'Shea's was, at this hour, the only place still open. He squinted at the meter on the cab and forked over the money to the driver, a silent man who sported a name, according to his ID, that contained no vowels. The cab was pricey, but Paley had made decent wages at the museum that day, so he decided he could afford it. Because of his Braithwaite, Paley took cabs only rarely. He usually reserved such an extravagance for a night like tonight, when he didn't want to risk damaging his good linen suit.

Paley slammed the door of the cab and headed toward the bar. Someone had affixed a poster to the brick wall outside that read FREE SQUEAKY FROMME; beside it was another reading FREE PEDICURES AND LEG WAXING. Manhattan. He shook his head and went inside.

As soon as Paley pushed open the door of O'Shea's, he knew he could rule out the dress-code idea. The bartender himself was in shirtsleeves, a white towel hanging from his considerable waist. Judging by how they were dressed, the customers at the bar seemed to include an off-duty doorman, the driver of a hansom cab, and a sanitation engineer. They all looked lost in Jay Leno's monologue on the TV at the far end of the bar, but each glanced up just long enough to size up the newcomer. There wasn't a menacing face in the room, but Paley couldn't shake the notion that he was unwelcome here. It was like the moment when a stranger walks into a saloon in a western: everyone just stares. For his part, Paley wished he were back in his apartment, in his boxers, dancing around the living room to the B-52's.

"Paley," came a whisper from behind. He turned to find Herzog huddled in a corner of a booth that Paley hadn't even noticed. Herzog, too, was wearing a suit, though in this light it seemed to be threadbare—something that Herzog might have purchased during his last flush period, which, from the wide collars and abundance of pockets, Paley figured to have been during the midseventies. Propped beside Herzog on the seat was a huge black briefcase.

"So," Paley said, hoping to open the conversation on a simple note, "you trying to sell me some Amway products?"

"No," Herzog said, unsmiling.

"Okay," said Paley. "My move. You brought me out here tonight and told me to wear a suit because . . ." Here he faltered, but Herzog said nothing. "Maybe you didn't mean a *suit* suit," Paley continued, "but something weird, instead. Like a suit of armor, or a bathing suit?"

"That's good," Herzog said, allowing himself a tiny, tense smile. "But not good enough."

"Okay," Paley said. "But it's got *something* to do with this place." Herzog still said nothing. Paley's eyes roved the booth, taking in the empty glass, the coaster, the bowl of mixed nuts that was mostly pared down to everyone's least favorite: filberts—anything that might be a clue. "You live near here?" he finally asked.

"Yes," said Herzog, and then he leaned forward, arms crossed on the oily tabletop. "Look," he continued, "I know you're humoring me. I know you didn't come here to play any game."

"So you tell me," Paley said. "Why did I come here?"

"Because you heard something in my voice on the phone," said Herzog. "Anxiety. Fear. And you couldn't help looking into it. Am I getting warm?"

"That's part of it," Paley said. "So what's the story?" he asked lightly.

"Somebody," Herzog said in the quietest of whispers, "is trying to kill me."

"I see." Paley looked beyond Herzog to the electric waterfall clock over the bar. He'd been here only three minutes, and already he wanted to leave.

"No, you don't *see*," said Herzog. "You're just trying to humor me. You think I'm just some fucking show-biz whiz-kid has-been who's been sitting alone in his room too long."

"No," said Paley. "That's what I think *I* am."

"Well, you're wrong," Herzog said, steamrolling past the attempt at a joke. "I'm not."

"Okay, okay," said Paley. Just then the bartender appeared at the end of the table.

"Two glasses of your best scotch," said Herzog. Paley raised a hand to object, but Herzog quickly said not to worry, it was *his* treat. But Paley turned to the bartender and firmly said, "I'll have a 7-Up." The bartender retreated.

"I never would have taken you for a teetotaler," said Herzog.

"Me neither," said Paley, and he let it drop.

The bartender brought over their drinks along with two cocktail napkins that had smutty party jokes printed on them. Paley took a swallow of carbonation and said, "So, where were we? Oh, yes. Somebody is trying to kill you."

"Not just me. All of us," said Herzog.

"Us?"

"The Mental Midgets," Herzog said, tapping his fingers on the tabletop, impatient at having to waste time on what seemed to him obvious. And maybe, Paley supposed, it *was* obvious—to someone in Herzog's state of mind.

"You're starting to give me the creeps," Paley said.

"Good," said Herzog. "Now maybe you'll listen. I've talked to everybody about this, all the Mental Midgets, even the Professor. But nobody wants to hear it. Everybody would rather just stay blind to the facts. Maybe you could talk to them. Maybe they'd listen to *you.*"

"And what," Paley said, clearing his throat, "are the facts?"

Herzog held out his palm and started counting on his fingers. "First, Larry Kelleher is killed in a home accident. Then today, *I'm* almost killed. At home. By accident."

"Could be coincidence," Paley said evenly.

"I calculated the odds," said Herzog. "Do you know what the chances are that two members of a six-person group would die within a couple of weeks of each other, factoring in first the statistical probability that *both* fatalities would occur in the home, then the statistical probability that both home fatalities would be *accidental?* Do you know what those chances *are?*"

"Not offhand."

"Astronomical!"

"It's possible, I suppose," Paley offered.

"It's more than possible. It's the truth. Like today, I'm in my apartment, racing around and frantically closing the blinds before the window washers show up outside, when what should I find under my desk but *this.*" Herzog searched through three of his jacket's outside pockets before producing what appeared to be an electrical plug. This he slapped triumphantly on the table.

Paley picked it up. It *was* an electrical plug. "I'm afraid I don't follow you," he said.

"The wires. Look at the wires," urged Herzog.

Paley did. The tiny twisted wires were frayed. He shrugged. "Wires wear out," he said.

"Yeah, yeah, I know all that," said Herzog. "But they also *start fires*. You don't have to be Thomas Edison to see that these wires have been pared back. With pliers. They've been deliberately exposed."

"Or gnawed on," said Paley, and he absently began shredding his napkin.

"What are you saying? I've got rats?" said Herzog. He looked terribly offended.

"Well, no," said Paley. "I mean, I don't know the vermin factor in your apartment; I've never been there. All I'm saying is there might be a reasonable explanation, even one that beats the astronomical odds. I'm sorry, Herzog, but I'm not convinced."

Paley absently glanced down at his napkin. He'd ripped

it in pieces right in the middle of a joke; now all he could read was the punch line: " 'Why sir,' said the flustered stewardess, 'if I'd known *that,* I would have brought you your coffee hours ago!' " Paley crumpled up the remainder of the napkin and pushed it aside. "And even if I *were* convinced," he went on, "we'd still have two big questions: Who? And why? A suspect. And a motive."

Herzog slumped back. He seemed to be retreating, his eyes narrowing. Paley suddenly wondered if his old friend's paranoia ever manifested itself in moments of violence. "A motive," said Herzog in a weary voice. "You're right. Why would anyone want to kill a bunch of has-beens—no offense, Paley—a bunch of fucking *consultants.* You know," he said, shaking his head, "if our parents had known we were going to end up like this, I don't think they would have been so eager to send us out on national TV." He shook his head. "Maybe Tony Minion did Dora Bunyan a favor when he canned her. Maybe he saved her from a life of *nothingness.*"

Paley shrugged. "Or maybe she got incredibly depressed when she was canned and never recovered. Who ever knows that sort of thing?"

Even now, sitting and looking across the table at Davy Herzog, Paley realized that he would never have predicted Davy would wind up like this. Somehow, he would have imagined that Herzog's childhood paranoia would have been put to good use; it might have made him an excellent consumer advocate, for example, someone who ferrets out the ways in which big conglomerates try to screw the little guy. Instead, Herzog was a hopeless neurotic gripped by an unnatural fear of death.

"Look," said Paley, "if it will do any good, I'll call the others for you. I'll impress upon them how serious you were when you called them. And I'll make sure they're okay, that their lives aren't in any danger. Will that do the trick?"

"It would mean an awful lot to me," Herzog said, then he brightened. "What do you say we get out of this dump?" This sounded like the first sane suggestion Paley had heard all evening, and he quickly agreed. But then, as they were leaving the bar, Herzog turned back to Paley, and Paley saw the old fear returning to his eyes.

"I know this is going to sound crazy to you," Herzog said, forcing a smile. "But would you walk me home?"

Paley figured it was the least he could do. Besides, he still had several unanswered questions nagging at the back of his mind. For instance, what kind of apartment would Herzog possibly live in? How would it be decorated—Early Dustball? What did Herzog do all day? Did he have any friends? Herzog seemed like a man whose generic paranoia was much more clear-cut than any of the *specifics* of his life. The only image Paley could summon up was of Herzog racing around to close the blinds before the window washer arrived at the window. But why? This image seemed so extreme—but then again, everything about Herzog seemed extreme. And nothing, somehow, seemed quite real. It might all be attributed to pure—or impure—paranoia, Paley supposed.

"Glad to walk you home," he said now, and he meant it. He and Herzog set off together down the broad, quiet street. Paley liked walking around at this time of night. An empty bus ambled past; the city looked asleep. And if you weren't one of the lucky ones safe at home, turning back the covers and slipping into bed, then you might be one of the unlucky ones, pacing your dreary room, lonely tonight and always alone, like Herzog. Walking around at this time of night kept you suspended somewhere between both possibilities.

"You know," Herzog said after they'd walked in silence to the end of the block, "maybe you're right. I mean, sometimes I think I've got to get out of my room more often. I can get a little carried away, you know?"

"I know," said Paley.

Herzog inhaled deeply. "Night air in New York," he said. "Smells good. Well," he said, and then he stopped walking, "here we are."

Paley was surprised that they had reached Herzog's home already. He had expected something of a walk, but Herzog turned out to be living on the same block as O'Shea's. Herzog's building, in fact, looked like an office building. The marble lobby was bathed in fluorescent light, and a green directory of occupants hung on a wall. Two of the three elevator doors were open, their cars dark for the night.

"Thanks for all your help," Herzog said. He pressed the night bell next to the locked revolving doors; somewhere deep in the building a buzzer sounded.

"Oh, it was nothing," Paley said.

"I'll try to keep in mind what you said," Herzog went on. "About it all being a coincidence and everything."

"Do that," said Paley.

A soft *ding* came from inside the lobby, and a night watchman stepped out of the one operating elevator, his eyes small from sleep. While he crossed the lobby, he produced from his belt a key ring as big as a bagel.

"Well, good night," said Herzog, extending the hand that wasn't holding his briefcase.

"Good night," said Paley, surprised at Herzog's sudden formality, but shaking his hand anyway. The hand, not surprisingly, was cold and moist. Paley watched as Herzog turned away toward the door that the guard was unlocking; for days, he suspected, he would have trouble shaking the image of a condemned man being led back to his cell after visiting hours. Paley wiped his hand discreetly on a tissue from his pocket and began to walk away, but after only a second he wheeled around.

"Wait!" he called back. Herzog and the guard turned around in the building lobby. "I'm sorry, Mr. Herzog," Paley called through the glass, "but there's one matter of business we haven't concluded."

The Extra Credit Question is:

What Did Paley Mean?

(Solution on next page)

∫olution

"I almost forgot about the game," Paley said when Herzog had joined him on the sidewalk again.

"You used to be quicker," said Herzog, shaking his head. He glanced anxiously back at the guard, who was waiting with his arms crossed behind the closed lobby door.

"I said 'almost,' " Paley said. "The part about the suit had me confused for a while. I kept asking myself, Why should I have to dress up to meet you at some dive bar?"

"Good question," Herzog agreed.

"And then this neighborhood," Paley said. "It all looks like office buildings, so I had to keep asking myself, Where could Herzog possibly live?"

"Another good question."

"And then," Paley said, lowering his voice, "there was the matter of your hiding from the window washer. That should have given it away."

Should have, but didn't. What Paley had mistakenly dismissed as an extension of Herzog's paranoia was in fact a necessary precaution. Even now Herzog was glancing over his shoulder again at the lobby guard, as if the guard somehow could hear their whispered words through the plate glass of the lobby door—an ambiguous gesture on Herzog's part, Paley understood now, easily interpreted as paranoia, pure or impure. But what if it was necessary? Why would Herzog not want the lobby guard to overhear their conversation?

"Why would you *not* want a window washer to see the inside of your apartment?" Paley asked. "For the same reason you would want a lobby guard to see you in a suit. For the same reason you would want a lobby guard to see you talking to a friend in a suit. For the same reason you would want a lobby guard to think you're a businessman returning to your office to burn the midnight oil."

Herzog was silent. He merely tilted his face toward Paley, a smile slowly forming. For a moment he looked like the young Herzog, a kid enjoying a simple game.

"Because," Paley said, *"you're living in an office you've illegally converted to a residential apartment."*

"All right, all right," Herzog said, shushing Paley. "That's enough, Einstein. Don't say anything else. I take it back."

"Take it back?" Paley said, but Herzog was already trotting away. When he reached the lobby, the guard swung the door wide.

"You're just as quick as you ever were, Jack Paley," Herzog called as he vanished into his cellblock, leaving Paley alone on the sidewalk. Now it would be Paley's turn to pace the streets, to hail a cab, to return to an empty apartment. For just a moment, he thought longingly of O'Shea's, wishing that he were back there, even with Herzog—a couple of boys who'd come out to play.

Chapter Five
MURDER IN WONDERLAND

LIKE many geniuses, Paley didn't start talking until he was three years old, though he did watch a lot of television. Just when his parents started to think he might be a little dense, Paley looked up from his dinner plate one evening and suddenly announced, "Come to where the flavor is." The next day, Walter and Jean Paley had their son's IQ tested, and Jack was found to be in the 99th percentile. Years later, when auditions were held for "The Mental Midgets," no one doubted that he would land a slot on the show. Not only was he brilliant, but by second grade he was also tall and long-lashed and photogenic. For seven years he had correctly answered a battery of questions under hot klieg lights every Tuesday evening, but now, as an adult, there was a question in his head that even he couldn't begin to answer: *What if Herzog was right?*

The question had plagued him for days, following him around like a pop song he couldn't dislodge from his head. It could make its presence known anywhere—riding on his Braithwaite or running in Central Park or, Tuesday evening, right in the middle of foreplay. "Where'd you go?" Belinda asked, propping herself up on her elbow, and it took him a moment to realize that where he'd gone was Herzog's apartment, a place Paley imagined to be as cluttered and dark and full of firetraps as Herzog's mind. Soon Paley was wondering about Tracy and Olive and Steve. While Belinda tried to bring Paley back by rubbing his back and buttocks with some vanilla-scented "love oil" she'd bought at a little sex shop in the Village ("I thought it was a toiletries store," she'd told him, "and I thought I'd buy some soap-on-a-rope for you, but the next thing I knew I was surrounded by edible underwear"), was there someone following Tracy home down Avenue B, or cornering Olive in a stairwell, or standing over Steve as he peacefully dreamed of Nautilus equipment? Or was Herzog waking up to a wall of fire? And what about Paley—was someone even now creeping past Mrs. Cellini's apartment and toward his? What if Herzog *was* right?

Paley sat up in bed, his body coated with vanilla slime. "I'm sorry," he said to Belinda. "I'm not much good tonight. But I'd be happy to do *you*," he volunteered.

"Do me?" Belinda said, offended. "I didn't know I could be *done*."

"You know what I mean," Paley said, but already she was climbing down the ladder of the loft bed.

"Some other time," she called up to him. "I want a lover who's there in mind *and* hand. Maybe it's just as well," she added, pulling on her robe. "You said that you're having a strenuous week, and you should probably get to sleep early."

It was true. This week, Paley was a housepainter— not the kind who simply washes walls with brushes, but someone who treats blank surfaces as if they were canvases. He'd had experience at such work years before. At boarding school he'd been a set painter, and years later, when he resettled in New York City after college, he'd made some extra money as a self-styled "apartment artist." Once, on the wall of a cramped bathroom in the West Village, he'd created a trompe l'oeil sink and shower; to the floor of a Flatiron loft he'd added a front lawn. He'd even endowed an airshaft in TriBeCa with the view from a penthouse overlooking Central Park. This week, he was adding a marble fireplace to a lower Fifth Avenue apartment that already had everything but.

"Please be *very* careful," Calvin Skinner, a prematurely white-haired man in a black kimono, had said as he'd led Paley through the apartment. "You'll be working in my study, and you must be absolutely scrupulous with the equipment there. I take great pride in my stereo and video accoutrements; they're my playthings —my hobbies, if you will—but I take them very seriously."

"Don't worry," Paley said, "I'll be careful." *And quick,* he added to himself. Already Paley couldn't wait to leave. Belinda's father had overheard Skinner at the Cavalry Club pining for a fireplace, and he'd suggested that Skinner call Fly-By-Night and request Paley's services as a painter. Still, Paley couldn't believe that Stewart Frank actually counted someone like Calvin Skinner among his friends. Something seemed wrong here. Maybe it was the place, a control freak's idea of heaven: a track-lighting system that brightened automatically as the sun started to set, a climate-adjustment device that monitored the temperature in tenths of degrees, a state-of-the-art home entertainment system in the study where Paley would be painting. Or maybe it was Calvin Skinner: clutching a cup of espresso and feigning boredom, yet all the same making sure that even a casual visitor such as Paley knew where every dollar in the place had gone. The only extravagance Skinner didn't bother to point out was the huge photograph over the white leather couch in the living room. The subject was a young girl. She looked about eleven or twelve years old, she was standing in a field of wheat, and she was naked. The edges of her hair barely covered her tiny breasts. The inscription on a plaque above the photo read, "Alice: Photographs by the Reverend Charles Dodgson." High-tech equipment, Paley thought, quickly looking away, might not be Calvin Skinner's only hobby. Then Paley felt Skinner watching him, anticipating his embarrassment, actually *enjoying* it.

Paley would soon learn that Skinner was always watching him. On Monday, his first day on the job, Paley found that he couldn't take a coffee break or even his lunch without receiving a visit from Skinner, who would just happen to be walking past the study. It was less stressful, Paley figured, simply to finish the job and be gone, and he soon stopped taking breaks. But on Wednesday, Paley decided that the time had come to keep his promise to Davy Herzog and check on the other Mental Midgets. After asking Skinner for permission to use the phone, Paley sat behind the desk in the study and called Tracy.

When she answered, Paley thought her voice might have sounded distant, timorous, cautious.

"What's wrong?" Paley said. "My God, there *is* something wrong."

"Who *is* this?" The voice had shifted, from faint to alert, and Paley could hear another voice in the background, a woman urging Tracy to hang up if it was an obscene caller.

"It's me, Paley. You sounded like there's something wrong."

"Oh, Paley," she said, laughing. "No, I was just busy. What is this, Scare the Shit Out of Tracy Selwyn Week?"

"Sorry," he said. Then, "What do you mean?"

"First Davy Herzog, and now you."

Paley laughed. "Yeah, you know Herzog. Still crazy after all these years. Herzog, actually, is the reason I'm calling."

"Look," Tracy said, "can I call you back or something?"

"You're not alone," Paley said, "right?"

"You always were the quickest Midget," she said dryly.

Paley had to smile. Last night he'd worried how the other Mental Midgets were faring while he went about his love life, and now it turned out that they were simply going about their own.

"I can't talk long, either," Paley said. "But I just wanted to make sure you're okay. Herzog has this idea about the Midgets being somehow . . . *threatened*. You know what I mean; he said he'd called you."

"Listen, as I told Davy, I'm fine, couldn't be better. Honest," Tracy said. "It's sweet of you to call, but I really have to go now." And the last sound Paley heard, before the click of the receiver, was a duet of giggles.

Steve Carrera was next. His machine picked up, and Steve's wooden voice began to drone, but while Paley was leaving his name, Steve's real voice came on the line.

"Hey, Paley! Don't hang up!" There was a shriek of feedback, then the hoofbeats of Steve's fumbling with the phone and punching buttons on the answering machine. "I was just in the shower."

Paley offered to call back.

"No!" Steve said. "I'm glad to hear from you, I don't mind dripping a little."

"Well," Paley said, "here I am."

"I've been thinking about the old gang, too," Steve said, "ever since the memorial. I just can't get it out of my mind. Wondering how everybody is."

"Same here," Paley found himself agreeing. "So," he went on, "how *are* you?"

"Fine, fine," Steve said. "Things have been quiet."

"Nothing out of the ordinary?"

"You know, Davy Herzog called and asked me the same thing. Babbled on about how we should be extra careful; it was weird. *Should* something be wrong?"

"You know Herzog," said Paley. "Always the worrier. But I told him I'd call everyone again, just to check in."

"Well, I'm great, great," said Steve. "Couldn't be better." This was the second time in a minute that Paley had heard from a Mental Midget that his or her life couldn't be better. Was it just *his* life, then, that could use a little sprucing up? "You know, this idea occurred to me, after Larry's memorial service?" Steve said. "I thought maybe we could all get together, the Mental Midgets. You know, like a reunion."

A reunion: Hadn't they just *had* one? The idea of seeing the other Midgets again was too much for Paley; it was too soon. In a year, maybe, he'd feel differently.

"Maybe," Paley told him. "Maybe sometime, Steve."

"Or just the two of us," said Steve. "You know, no big deal. Just you and me, for coffee or something. You know, ever since the memorial service I've been thinking about those times we had together back then, on the show. Goofing around, studying, getting fan mail. And you know, those seem like the best times of our lives. I mean, I can't speak for you, but it was for me. My best time, I mean. You know?"

Paley was silent. "I know," he finally said.

"I could come down to your neighborhood," Steve said.

"I can't," Paley said. "I just can't," he went on, searching for a reason to tell Steve. "I don't have my calendar with me," Paley said, coming up with the one excuse that any true New Yorker wouldn't question.

"Oh."

"But I'll call you back," Paley said. "Okay?"

"Sure. Hey, no problem," Steve said. But before Paley could say good-bye, Steve went on, "Say, you don't by any chance have Tracy's number, do you?"

Paley gave him the number, but urged him not to use it for at least another hour.

Which left only Olive Herne. When he dialed her number and got a busy signal, Paley was tempted to abandon his promise to Herzog and return to his work. He gazed into the fireplace; the last thing he'd been painting was a poker in the corner. It looked odd, bloated, from this distance; Paley saw now that he'd lavished so many layers of paint on the poker that it had swelled to the size of a baseball bat—evidence, no doubt, of his distraction with the phone calls to the Mental Midgets. He could expand the poker into a bellows, he supposed; he could trim it back into a poker; he could call Olive. Paley punched the redial button on the phone console, and this time his call went through.

"It's Paley," he said, and the line seemed to hum while this news sank in.

What was the worst that could happen? Paley asked himself. That she would call him by one of his old nicknames, and he would get excited? He hadn't thought of these names in years, but now they both came back. The derivation of "Stretch" had been obvious. The other one, though, had taken a little explaining. The time during the final season when he and Olive had exploratorily French-kissed backstage, Paley had finally worked up the courage to ask her why she sometimes called him Orion.

"It's a constellation," she'd whispered. "Of a great hunter."

They were squeezed together on the Naugahyde couch in the green room. In one hand Paley balanced her braid, in the other her unsnapped rubber band. He was uncertain where to go from here.

"So?"

"So, silly," she said, "you find Orion by looking for his sword and his belt."

Their romance had never progressed past that one memorable moment, which itself was interrupted moments later by the Professor's unannounced arrival in the doorway, but it wasn't for lack of Olive's trying. She'd walk ahead of Paley down the studio hallway, wagging her developing hips, or she'd run her fingers through his hair one second before the Mental Midgets went onstage, prompting Paley's first encounter with on-camera flop-sweat.

Although he had been Olive's type, he hadn't been Olive's mother's type. Imperious but anxious, her hair swept back under a scarlet scarf, she'd often stood just out of camera range beside Tony Minion during the tapings, chewing a fingernail whenever a question came her daughter's way, waiting for a commercial break so she could swoop down on the set and thumb an imaginary smudge off Olive's face. Around the set she had earned the nickname of the Widow Herne; her husband had died soon after Olive was born, and she now devoted her life exclusively to her daughter. The Widow Herne regarded Paley—regarded all the Mental Midgets, and probably most of humanity—with a formal distance that wasn't impolite but that nonetheless carried a single unmistakable message: My daughter is too good for you. Over the years Paley had occasionally daydreamed about Olive, wondering what might have happened between them if her mother hadn't always been in the way. What would it have been like to fall in love with another Mental Midget? What would it have been like to spend his adult life with someone who really understood the pressures and disappointments of having once been a child prodigy?

It would have been wonderful. But the romance between Paley and Olive was not in the stars—at least, not in the Widow Herne's stars. Olive's mother had her own romance, though. A year after "The Mental Midgets" went off the air, the society page of the *Times* carried the news that producer Tony Minion had wed Sybil Herne. So now Olive was Tony Minion's stepdaughter, and it was probably best that Paley and Olive had never become a real item: Sunday dinners at the Minion-Herne household would have been too much to bear. Elbows off the table, debates about Wittgenstein during dessert. Olive still knew how to flirt, though. For an excruciating amount of time she paused now on the other end of the telephone; Paley could hear her breathe.

"I knew you'd call," she finally said.

"I really can't talk, but I told Herzog I'd see how you were doing. How all of you are doing."

"Much better," she said, "now that you've called. Actually, life has been great lately." Great, Paley thought—again with the *great*. Just how great could these geniuses be doing if Paley could locate them all at home on a weekday afternoon? "I've had some wonderful news," Olive went on. "Do you want to guess?"

"Does it have to do with your newspaper column?"

"Yes! How did you know?"

"Just lucky," Paley said.

"Well, go on."

"I can't, Olive. I really can't stay on the phone."

"Oh, go on, Paley. One more guess isn't going to hurt. I bet you can do it."

Paley bit his lip. "Does it have to do with finding a wider audience?" he said after an appropriate pause.

"Wow," she said. "Did somebody tell you?"

"You yourself said it was good news," Paley said. "If it has to do with your newspaper column, the good news can't be a *diminished* audience. It's simple."

"Simple for you, Stretch," she said. "Go on, go on."

Paley closed his eyes. He continued until he'd "guessed" what he'd already heard from Herzog at the memorial service—that Olive was being given her own daily show on MTV.

"You see?" Olive said. "I *told* you you'd get it. You're so smart. Nothing's changed, has it?"

But that was just it: Everything had changed, though Paley didn't have the nerve to tell her. Already she was plowing ahead with her own revised version of the past.

"I found it exciting to see the old faces again at poor Larry Kelleher's memorial service. Some of us have fared better than others, of course. But you and I, Paley, we still look good. Don't you find it moving, talking to someone with whom you shared certain intimacies so many years ago?"

"I suppose," he said. "Although they weren't all that intimate, Olive."

"Intimate enough," she said.

"I suppose."

"They've kept *me* thinking, over the years."

"Have they?"

"Haven't *you* thought about them?" she said. "Be honest."

"I suppose I have." Paley cleared his throat.

"There you go," she said. "Now was that so difficult? We're all grown-up, Paley, we can talk about these things." She paused. "We can do these things."

"Yes, well."

"Well, *well*."

"How's your mother?" Paley said suddenly.

But before Olive could answer, Paley was interrupted

by Calvin Skinner. He paced past the doorway to the study, smiling weakly.

"I have to go," Paley said. "I'll call."

"Sure you will."

"Honest I will," Paley said. "You're right. It might be nice to see each other again."

"You don't have to lie to me, Paley. I'm a big girl now, I can handle rejection."

"Nobody can handle rejection," Paley said, "but that's beside the point. I'm at work, and I've got to go."

"What kind of work?"

"Consulting," Paley said after a moment, and he hung up.

"I hope I didn't hurry you," Calvin Skinner said, instantly reappearing in the doorway and sweeping into the room. He was holding a cigarette over an azure bowl. As he spoke, he flicked ash. "But I *do* have to use the phone, and I *have* been waiting out there forever."

"Sorry," Paley said, getting up from the chair behind the desk.

"That's quite all right." Skinner took one last deep drag on the cigarette before crushing it in the bowl. "I'm sure you wouldn't have kept me waiting to use my own phone if it weren't for something urgent."

Skinner picked up the receiver, and Paley turned to the faux fireplace. A giant poker wasn't the only thing he'd painted into a corner; now he'd have to call Olive *again*, and this time there would be no mistaking his intentions. The only problem was, what *were* his intentions? Even if he was attracted to Olive, was it to the Olive of today, or to the braided, breathy Olive of fourteen? Another minute on the phone with her, and he might have known. If only Calvin Skinner hadn't needed to make a call at just that moment.

"Cool and clear tonight," Skinner announced now, hanging up the phone, "low in the midfifties, and positively no mention of rain. One must prepare what to wear for one's evening," he added, laughing.

Paley didn't turn around. He pretended to be lost in thought about the fireplace. Skinner's laughter stopped abruptly.

"That poker is *plump*," Calvin Skinner said. Paley turned around in time to see the back of Skinner's head disappear out the doorway, and for just a moment Paley entertained a fantasy of tapping him on the bean with that poker, if only it were real.

In fact, it *was* a blow to the head that killed Calvin Skinner.

The news greeted Paley the next morning when he showed up for work. The doorman to Skinner's building hopped off his stool when he noticed Paley walking his Braithwaite into the vestibule.

"Say, you can't go up," the doorman said, stepping forward gingerly. He presented this information not so much as a warning but as a fact, almost as if he were eager to share it with someone.

"Why not?" Paley said.

"It's Mr. Skinner," the doorman said. "He's passed away."

The doorman's eyebrows arched as he studied Paley's reaction.

"Natural causes?" Paley said.

"How well did you know him?"

Paley shrugged. "Not well," he said.

"You weren't a friend or nothing?"

"Just doing some decorating."

The doorman nodded his head hungrily, then looked both ways as if he was about to let Paley in on a secret he'd been dying to share all morning.

"He was *bludgeoned*," he said.

Paley leaned his bicycle against the wall.

"Isn't that something?" the doorman went on. "Just like that. Not that I didn't see it coming. I mean, with all due respect to the deceased and everything, Mr. Skinner was not what you'd call your typical tenant."

"Bludgeoned," Paley murmured.

"A hammer in the head," the doorman said, absently scratching the back of his own head. "That'll do it every time, you bet."

"Do the police know who did it?"

The doorman shrugged. "You go for a walk in Washington Square Park in the middle of the night, you're not exactly making it easy on the cops."

Just then an elevator door opened and two police officers emerged, a man with a barrel gut and red hair, and a tall black woman. The doorman and Paley stepped aside, but the policewoman stopped and regarded Paley.

"By any chance, are you here to see Calvin Skinner?" she said.

Paley nodded and he explained about his work in the apartment. The doorman wandered to the other end of the foyer, whistling.

"Oh, so that was *your* painting," the officer said. "We'd wondered about that. I'm Sgt. Rose Belknap, and this is my partner Sgt. Milo Toomey. We'll need a statement from you." Sergeant Toomey seemed disappointed by this news; he shook his head, thrust his hands in the pockets of his black police windbreaker, and told Sergeant Belknap that he'd meet her outside. Sergeant Belknap stared after him as he walked out of the lobby.

"Partner trouble?" Paley asked.

"Nothing I can't handle," Sergeant Belknap said, and Paley believed her. Already she had her pen and notepad ready; she fired a series of questions at Paley: When had he last seen the victim? Did he have any reason to believe that the deceased was in danger? Had he witnessed any mysterious behavior around the Skinner apartment? Throughout the questioning, the rim of her cap hung low, but her eyes shone through the shadow, narrow, alert, predatory, like a tiger's; it would be difficult to imagine a situation Sergeant Belknap couldn't handle. Paley found himself studying the reflection in a mirror across the foyer: the tall, light Paley; the tall, dark Belknap. They were a striking couple, a much more intimidating presence than Belknap and Toomey.

"Maybe your partner was right," Paley said after a while. "I'm not being much help."

"Maybe my partner is waiting for his pension," said Sergeant Belknap. Then, "Sorry. That was uncalled for."

"Don't be sorry," said Paley. "It's understandable. It's even pleasantly unexpected."

Sergeant Belknap ignored this remark. Her by-the-book demeanor had returned. She asked if Paley had left any personal items in Skinner's apartment.

"A drop cloth," he said. "Some tools. And the fireplace, of course."

"Well, we've sealed off the apartment for the time being, so you'll have to fill out some paperwork when you want your belongings back. The tools, anyway. I don't know what to tell you about the painting."

Paley shrugged. "What you can tell me about," he said, "is this case."

"I'm sorry, but that is out of the question, Mr.—" And here she faltered. "I haven't asked for your name yet."

"Jack Paley," he said. "But most people just call me Paley."

"Address?" she said, writing down his name. Then she stopped. She looked up from her notepad, and the tiger eyes were gone. In their place was a sight that Paley witnessed every couple of years, the sight of someone receding inside, searching through old clippings, flipping past ancient channels.

"There used to be a Jack Paley," she said slowly. "On this TV show. The tall one," she added, sizing him up.

"There still is a Jack Paley," he said.

"Well, isn't this something." She took her cap off and smiled. "See?" she said. "Toomey leaves me alone, gets me so mad I forget to ask your name, and what does he miss out on but a Mental Midget."

Paley did what he always did when he found himself in this circumstance; he shrugged and smiled and tried not to look too young or too smug or too foolish.

"The Mental Midgets," Sergeant Belknap said, shaking her head. "You know," she said, "I didn't much care for that show."

Paley stopped trying to look humble.

"You can't blame me," she quickly added. "I'm sure it was a fine show. But I remember sitting there in front of the TV just mad as hell that I'd never get to be on it. Lots of kids would have loved to be on it, of course. Lots of kids dreamed about it. But the difference is that white kids at least knew they had a *shot.*"

It was true, of course; she was right. The all-white nature of the show was a reflection of a time in the country's history that some people might consider "innocent," but that Paley now regarded as "guilty." What first woke Paley up to the show's inherent racism was sophomore American Lit with Mr. Givens, a young teacher at boarding school who gave the class dramatic readings of *Soul on Ice.*

"I'm sorry about that," Paley said now. "I don't know what else to say."

"Nothing else *to* say," she said, placing her cap back on her head. "If it's any consolation, though, you *were* my favorite."

"So how about it?" he said. "Can you make an exception for your favorite Mental Midget and let me know something about this case?"

She glanced around the lobby. The doorman had returned to a stool in a corner, where he sat with his arms folded, his chin resting on his chest, his eyes closed. Toomey paced outside, under the building's awning, eating a package of Ho Ho's.

"Come on," Paley said.

"I can't," she said.

"But you want to."

She shrugged, shrinking inside her leather jacket. "I also wanted to be a Mental Midget."

"So here's your chance," Paley said. "Yes, now you, too, can match wits with a Mental Midget."

She smiled. Paley returned her smile. After a moment Sergeant Belknap looked around again, and then she leaned closer to Paley.

"All right," she said. "But I never told you any of this. Understand?"

He nodded.

"All we know," she said, "is this. Skinner leaves the building about twelve-forty last night and goes for a walk. About one o'clock a squad car on a routine patrol through the park finds his body on a bench on the west side of the square. The blood is fresh, the body's warm, and inside of five minutes another squad car pulls in this guy who claims he was just out for a stroll because he couldn't sleep. He says he didn't know Calvin Skinner, never heard of him, never spoke to him."

"So who's this guy?" said Paley.

"Sterling Ransom."

"Some guy." Paley let out a low whistle. "He could hire somebody to take his walks in the park for him."

"Last night he should have," said Sergeant Belknap.

"Then you've got a case, Sergeant?"

Sergeant Belknap smiled. "Call me Rose," she said, "and no, we don't have a case. Everybody we talk to says that these two didn't know each other. They belonged to the same private club, but a lot of people belong to private clubs. We have a murder weapon—a hammer found in a trash can on MacDougal Street—but no prints. Ransom *was* wearing gloves, but it was a cold night. If only we could establish a connection between the two men," she said, "then everybody would be happy."

"This club you mentioned," Paley said, "it wouldn't be the Cavalry Men's Club, would it?"

"You know it?"

"Of it," Paley said. "You want some help?"

"Well," she said, looking over her shoulder at the slumbering doorman, "officially it would be against all departmental procedure for me to encourage the involvement of a civilian in police business."

"And unofficially, Rose?"

"You're the genius," she said. "You figure it out."

"Give me a day," he said, "and I'll do my best. After all," he said, picking up his Braithwaite, "I'm temporarily out of work."

Belinda didn't like it when Paley showed up at her office unannounced, so he called her from a phone in the lobby of her father's Times Square office complex.

"What about our agreement?" she said. "Today's Thursday. I thought we sleep together only on Tuesday evenings."

"That's right," he said. "And I have no intention of sleeping with you now. Remember last week, Wednesday afternoon? We went to the movies, but we didn't literally *sleep* together. Besides," he said, "this week our Tuesday evening together wasn't exactly ideal."

"Wasn't consummated, you mean," she said. "So what am I supposed to say?"

"How about, 'Come on up, snookums, I can't wait to see you'? I'll make it worth your while," he pressed on. "Promise."

She sighed, and relented. A minute later Paley was closing Belinda's office door behind him and saying, "You'll never believe what happened." He perched on her desk and told her all about Skinner and the murder and the police sergeant—and the Cavalry Men's Club.

"That's why I had to see you," he said. "I know your father takes his lunch there every day. Beef Wellington, rare. It's a long shot, but if I can just get inside the club—"

"And you want my father to arrange it."

"Just past the door. I'll handle it from there."

"I'll bet you will." Belinda swiveled in her chair toward the window. "Just one question," she said. "Who is this woman lieutenant?"

"Sergeant," he said. "Nobody special. Don't be jealous."

"I'm not jealous." Belinda propped her legs on the window ledge in an approximation of nonchalance. "So," she said, playing with a few paper clips, "is she cute?"

"Cute? Nah," Paley said. "Besides, I make it a rule never to date anyone whose gun is bigger than mine."

"Filthy mouth," she said, and she folded her arms. "I don't know why I keep you around."

"Because I'm low maintenance?" Paley tried.

"Maybe."

"Because I have a way with words?"

She paused. "Yeah, you're a regular thesaurus," she said. "A real Roget."

Paley came around the desk and dropped to his knees beside her. He ran two fingers along the calf of her left leg, and she shivered. " 'Caress,' " he whispered. "A verb. Also, 'stroke,' 'massage,' or 'knead.' " He began to kiss the inside of her leg. The thin membrane of her nylon stockings was both exasperating and exciting.

"Paley," said Belinda, "what are you doing?" But her voice had a smoky quality to it that Paley knew to be an indication of arousal. She clasped her arms around him and pulled him closer. It was an awkward position, and the springs of her chair groaned like a mattress. "What if," Belinda said, her breath coming heavily, "someone sees?"

"It'll give them an education," he said, panting openly. "But no one *will* see." Paley's entire body was below window level. If anyone happened to look in, all they would see was a dressed-for-success woman leaning back in her chair, eyes glazed over happily, probably in the throes of some brilliant executive idea.

"Then what about my secretary?" she asked, her hands buried in his head of curls as though she were gathering yarn.

"Oh, she won't hear a thing," he murmured. "When I walked in, she was deep into a romance novel. *Love's Savage Seed*. Nothing could pull her away." Paley inched up Belinda's blue silk skirt, and Belinda slid lower in her chair.

"Oh, Roget," whispered Belinda. "Roget, don't stop."

So he didn't, not until Belinda's hand fell helplessly open and a torrent of paper clips began to rain down over Paley like an unexpected afternoon shower.

The Cavalry Club was the kind of place where even the busboys had all gone to Groton and Choate, where the waitresses had had coming-out parties that year. The only coming-out party Paley had ever attended was given by his friends Dennis and Garrison at their Bank Street apartment, but that was another story.

Usually, Paley wouldn't have so much as stepped

inside a club with an exclusionary policy. Under other circumstances, he might have joined the group of women parading their picket signs on the sidewalk in front of the club. "Sorry," was all Paley could say to these women as he wedged through the line. But he felt like a heel, a scab—a scab on somebody's heel.

"Sorry isn't good enough," called a frizzy-headed woman.

"Look, I'm not a member," Paley tried. "They wouldn't let me join if I were the last man on *earth*." But it did no good; three women were now starting to heckle him. He felt like Bobby Riggs trapped in the women's locker room at Wimbledon. Quickly, Paley slipped into the revolving door of the Cavalry Club; in a moment he was transported to a silent world of velvet drapes and golden light. The noise of the street outside disappeared as suddenly as if he'd slammed a sarcophagus lid.

Stewart Frank had agreed to meet Paley in the sitting room of the club that afternoon. After seeing Belinda at her office, Paley had gone home to change into his good suit. The hat-check clerk at the Cavalry directed Paley to the members' sitting room, where Stewart Frank barely looked up from the peach pages of the *Financial Times*.

"I'll have a refill," Stewart said, nodding toward the glass on the table beside him.

"Stewart?"

He looked up. "Oh, Jack," he said, getting to his feet and vigorously pumping Paley's hand. "You surprised me. I thought you were Stubbs." He looked around him, distracted. "Where *is* Stubbs, anyway?" he asked. "I need this freshened."

Paley pulled up a chair. He considered the room—the half-light that had filtered past the skyscrapers of Midtown Manhattan before settling through the full-length windows, the slow spirals of cigar smoke that rose from half a dozen standing ashtrays. As his eyes adjusted, Paley thought he could make out several faces familiar from the evening news or the front page—an unindicted coconspiring former presidential adviser here, a convicted inside trader there.

"What are you drinking?" Stewart said.

Paley shook his head. "Nothing, thanks," he said. "Actually, I came to see you about a favor."

"Belinda mentioned I might see you," Stewart said. "You know I'm always pleased to help out. I gave Calvin Skinner your name, after all. Although he won't be of much use to you anymore, I suppose."

"I was in the middle of the job when he died."

"Bad luck for you."

"For me?"

"Well, you'll never get paid now."

It was true, of course, but somehow it hadn't occurred to Paley until Stewart mentioned it. Paley had a good mind for a number of things, he told himself, but business would never be one of them.

"But you said something about a favor."

"Yes," Paley said. "You know how you're always saying there are certain advantages to knowing the right people?"

"Ah," Stewart said. "An introduction. For someone of your talents, a pleasure. Thinking of getting a real job?"

"Afraid not."

"Oh." Stewart looked disappointed. "Oh, well," he said after a moment. "You can't blame me for trying. So who is it you want to meet?"

"Sterling Ransom."

Stewart sank back in his chair. "That," he said, "might be a problem."

"You do know him?"

"I certainly know *of* him."

Stewart's eyes shifted slightly, and Paley turned to follow his line of sight to a corner of the room that seemed particularly animated. Several men had drawn their chairs together, partners in the same law firm perhaps, discussing the finer points of a difficult case as if circling the wagons. Then Paley realized that that's precisely what they had done—formed a protective circle around their old friend Sterling Ransom.

"Maybe this isn't such a good time to meet him, after all," said Paley.

"Maybe not," said Stewart. "Poor guy. That's an unfortunate situation he's found himself in. Still, I don't suppose anything will come of it," he added. "If the police think they can press charges against someone like Sterling Ransom—"

"Then you know him?" said Paley.

"I've already told you I don't," said Stewart. "Just because we're members of the same club hardly means we know each other. Certainly I've seen him here. And certainly I've nodded hello to him."

"What about Ransom and Skinner? Did they know each other, or were they merely nodding acquaintances?" Paley asked.

"Well," said Stewart, "let me think. I've certainly seen each of them in this room at the same time. And I suppose it's possible that they exchanged more than an occasional nod. But if you're asking if they were friends, then I'd have to say, to the best of my knowledge, the answer is no. What's this all about, anyway?"

"I'm not sure," Paley said. "For the time being, let's just call it the insatiable curiosity of the temporarily unemployed."

"You know, Jack," Stewart said, lowering his voice, "if you *do* ever need a real job—"

"Thanks," Paley said, "but a job where my employer gets murdered is about all the reality I can handle."

Stewart smiled. "Sometimes you remind me of me. Sometimes—" He stopped himself. "Don't take this the wrong way, Jack," he tried again, "but sometimes I can even imagine what it is my daughter sees in you."

"You a reporter?"

The doorman of the building on University Place where Sterling and Cicely Ransom owned a penthouse covered the mouthpiece of the phone and peered at Paley.

"Tell her I just saw her husband at the Cavalry," Paley said. The doorman, who had previously been eyeing Paley's bicycle with some suspicion, paused before relaying the message. Then he whispered into the telephone, "There's a man named Jack Paley here who *says* he just saw Mr. Ransom at the Club." He listened for a moment, then said, "I see," and looked up at Paley. "She wants to talk to you."

"I'm very sorry to disturb you now," Paley said into the lobby phone, "but I just wanted to tell you in person how aggrieved we all are."

"I see, Mr. Paley," said Cicely Ransom, and her voice was surprisingly breathy and young. In the excitement of the previous eight hours, Paley had forgotten the story behind Sterling and Cicely Ransom—how Ransom had been a less-than-lonely bachelor for most of his adult life until he'd shocked New York society by marrying the extremely young daughter of his rival in the copper-mining industry.

Cicely Neff had been a freshman at Smith when she became involved with Sterling Ransom. He would drive up to see her in Northampton on weekends. Other girls entertained skinny, earnest freshmen up from Princeton or down from Dartmouth for the weekend; Cicely entertained a middle-aged, Bentley-driving *man* in her room in Chapin House. He was old enough to be her father, everyone whispered in scandalized, titillated voices.

"Well," Cicely Ransom continued now, "if you're a member of the Cavalry Club, I guess it's okay to talk to you. But just for a minute."

"Thank you," Paley said, and he handed the doorman the phone. While the doorman received his instructions from Cicely Ransom, Paley folded the Braithwaite. The doorman snapped open the door to the lobby, and he even bowed slightly, as Paley carried his bicycle toward the elevator.

Paley didn't know what exactly he was hoping to find in the apartment of Sterling Ransom. He only knew that he had to act quickly, getting inside the penthouse before Sterling returned home. The visit to the Cavalry hadn't been helpful except to prove that Ransom and Skinner might in fact have met at the club. But that wasn't necessarily where they conducted their business—whatever it was. Still, if Paley couldn't find the crucial connection between Ransom and Skinner at the club, maybe he would find it in Ransom's home. He only hoped, as he watched the numbers in the elevator blink all the way up to PH, that he would know it when he saw it.

"Don't look at me," Cicely Ransom warned as the elevator doors opened directly into the penthouse. "I look like hell warmed over. I mean, I haven't even washed my hair today."

The photos in the gossip pages had not done Cicely Ransom justice. For her public appearances, she had apparently adopted the habit of applying layers of makeup. But now, in the entrance to her apartment, Cicely Ransom stood free of makeup, and it made her look ten years younger than the thirty she probably was. Her black silk blouse was tucked into her jeans, and on her right wrist she wore a single, thin band of gold.

"Pleased to meet you," Paley said. He leaned the

folded bicycle against a brass umbrella stand and shook Cicely's hand, and she indicated a plush brown couch. Behind the couch the rooftops and water towers of the West Village stretched as far as the river. Beyond the river, the buildings of New Jersey were silhouetted against a deepening sunset.

"Would you like some tea?" asked Cicely in her childlike voice. "We've got cranberry surprise, chamomile dreams, and something called sarsaparilla, but I think that one tastes lousy. Sterly likes it, though."

"Chamomile," said Paley, thinking he might get her out of the living room for a few minutes.

But Cicely merely inclined her head toward the kitchen door and said, "Marie."

A young woman with red, wispy hair and a spattering of freckles appeared in the doorway. "Yes, mum," she said in an accent that sounded Irish to Paley.

"Two teas," said Cicely. "Chamomile."

The maid nodded and disappeared, and Paley found himself alone again with Cicely. She sat in a chair opposite him, raised her eyebrows, and smiled, as if she were eager to hear whatever Paley had to say. Paley was eager to hear it, too, if only because he had no idea what it would be. He searched the room for inspiration. It was a handsome room, he noted with disappointment; *handsome,* after all, was not a word he would have used to describe Skinner's all-white, high-tech heaven. Here, earth colors dominated. Maybe Ransom had been telling the truth after all. Maybe the two men had nothing more in common than membership in the same men's club. Maybe nothing connected Calvin Skinner and Sterling Ransom except that they happened to be in the same park at the same time.

"I can't say how sorry I am that what happened . . . happened," Paley finally said.

"Yes," said Cicely.

"You must be exhausted from talking to the police."

"Oh," said Cicely, rolling her eyes, "you'll never know. The same questions, again and again. Where was Sterly last night? Did Sterly know Mr. Skinner? Did I ever hear Sterly mention Mr. Skinner's name?"

They were good questions, Paley had to admit.

"What did you tell them?" Paley said.

"The police? The truth, of course."

"Of course," Paley said. "It's always been my understanding that Sterling and Mr. Skinner were no more than nodding acquaintances."

"Yes, I guess you could say that," said Cicely. "Although I don't know if they ever even *nodded* to each other. I mean, Sterly talks a lot about the other men at the Club, but he's never once mentioned this Mr. Skinner. That's what I told the police."

"What about the other question?" Paley said. "The one about where Sterling was last night?"

"Oh, that. I told the police a million times: Sterly couldn't sleep, so he went out."

"Did he usually have trouble sleeping?"

But before Cicely could answer, Marie returned. She placed a tray on the table between Paley and Cicely and poured them each a cup of tea. After she'd gone, Paley said to Cicely, "You were saying?" She looked at him blankly. Paley reached for his cup of tea. "About your husband having trouble sleeping?" he said, then sipped.

"Are you a policeman, too?" Cicely asked. "You guys are everywhere!"

"No," said Paley. "I'm not a cop. Just an interested . . . party."

"Well, the answer to your question is sometimes yes, and sometimes no. Sterly always sleeps light, and once he gets up, he stays up."

Paley took another swallow of his tea, and then another. He sensed he was wearing out his welcome here.

He drained the tea quickly, and he was about to put it down when he noticed a painted design on the cup's bottom. It was a tiny, delicate drawing of a young girl, he realized when he looked closer—a young girl, completely naked. He blinked twice, recovering.

"And last night," Cicely was saying, "the phone rang and he got it, and it was only a wrong number, but that was it for Sterly's sleep. He said he was going out for a walk, and the next thing I knew, the police were calling to say they'd taken Sterly away."

"I'm so sorry," Paley said, trying to sound sympathetic. But the fact was, he couldn't take his eyes off the cup. Was this simply the latest trend among the affluent? Or was this the connection he'd been seeking?

"You noticed." The sound of Cicely's voice startled Paley. "Sterly loves it when people notice. Once the ambassador to Burma and his wife were here for a visit, and they drank pot after pot of herb tea and never once peered inside the cup. Sterly went nuts." Paley smiled uneasily. "You don't like it?" Cicely said.

"No, it's not that," said Paley. "It's very interesting, actually. Does Sterly—I mean your husband—have other examples of this kind of art?"

"Oh, yes." Cicely leapt to her feet. "Want to see something? It's my husband's prize possession."

"Certainly," said Paley, and he followed Cicely out of the living room. She led him to a door off the main hall. When she opened it and turned on the light, Paley found himself inside Sterling's study.

And there on the wall of the room was a photograph of a young girl scantily clothed in Victorian costume. It was a similar photograph to the one Paley remembered from Skinner's apartment; the poses were close enough that the two photographs might have been part of a set. And then Paley noticed, at the top of the photo in Sterling Ransom's study, an inscription on a plaque: "Alice: Photographs by the Reverend Charles Dodgson."

Rose agreed to meet Paley in the lobby of Skinner's building.

"I left as soon as you called," she said as she strode into the vestibule.

"Where's your partner?"

"That's just what I need: Toomey finding out I'm getting help from a civilian. So, what do you have for me?"

"You said I could come by to pick up my tools sometime," Paley said. Rose stopped suddenly. She stared at him evenly. "Just a joke," Paley said, forcing a smile. "Can we go upstairs? I'll explain on the way."

Rose shrugged. "Only for a Mental Midget would I do this," she muttered, and the doorman opened the door.

During the elevator ride, Paley told her about the photographs he'd seen in both apartments, and she agreed that they might be a lead.

"But is that it?" she said. "I mean, I like that you're taking this so seriously. But it's nothing you couldn't have told me over the phone. And it's hardly solid evidence."

"But you did say that you've sealed off the apartment?" Paley said.

"Yes."

"So nothing in the apartment has been touched, right?"

"Nothing," she said as the elevator doors parted.

"In that case, I think I might be able to give you solid evidence." They stepped into the hall and walked toward Skinner's apartment. With a pocketknife Rose slit the red-and-white police seal across the doorframe. "There's a chance I can prove that there was a connection between Sterling Ransom and Calvin Skinner. And that," Paley added, brushing past her eagerly and entering the apartment, "is why I asked you here."

The Extra Credit Question is:

How Did Paley Prove the Connection?

(Solution on next page)

Solution

"Let's assume," said Paley as he led Rose through Skinner's apartment, "that Ransom and Skinner knew each other more than Ransom is letting on. Let's also assume that their 'similar artistic taste'—and I use the phrase very loosely—was more than coincidence. Let's assume they *had* conducted some business together, only it wasn't the kind of business they were free to discuss in public, at the Cavalry, or even with a wife, like Cicely."

"I follow you so far," she said, glancing at the photograph of a naked girl on the living room wall. "In fact, we've already uncovered several boxes of soft-core child pornography in this apartment. But a smart guy like Ransom, with the right lawyer, should be able to explain it all away."

"Not if we confront him with hard evidence that contrary to what he's said, he and Skinner *had* been in contact with each other on the night of the murder," said Paley. He paused outside Skinner's study. "Has anything been touched here?"

"No."

"Good." Paley crossed to Skinner's desk. "I spoke

to Ransom's wife this afternoon, and she told me that a wrong number is what woke her husband up last night.''

"She told me that, too. So?''

"But she only has her husband's word for it,'' said Paley. "What if it wasn't a wrong number? What if it was Skinner, breaking their gentlemen's agreement by calling Ransom at home?''

"What if?'' said Rose. "Are you saying I should get a warrant to check the phone company's records?''

"You could do that,'' said Paley. "Or you could simply do *this.*''

And he reached across Skinner's desk and pointed to the redial button on the phone—the same button Paley had used when calling Olive.

"If Skinner did call Ransom and then went outside immediately and was killed, then the last number he dialed should *still be stored inside this phone.* And if it *is* Ransom's number—''

"—then we've got our connection,'' said Rose. She picked up the phone, looked at Paley, and said, "Here goes.'' Then she hit the redial button.

Paley leaned his head into the receiver, pressing against the earpiece. After two rings, someone picked up the phone.

"Hello,'' said a young female voice on the other end, a voice with an Irish accent. "Ransom residence.''

Rose hung up.

"So the Mental Midget powers of reasoning still work,'' she said.

"And this makes you an honorary Mental Midget.''

"I guess it'll have to do.'' She took out a notepad and started scribbling in it. "I'll handle it from here, Paley. But I really appreciate your help.''

"Hey, no problem.'' He waited, but she didn't glance up. "Well, I should probably head home,'' he said.

She slapped shut her notepad and looked at Paley.

"What about you?" he said.

"My work's just beginning. First I've got to stop at the precinct and pick up a warrant and Toomey and probably a couple of backup officers. Then I've got to head over to Ransom's place and make the arrest. And then back to the precinct to book him and write up the paperwork."

"And then?"

"And then, I have a home to head to," she said. "A daughter, if that's what you mean."

"It is."

"I'm divorced, if that's also what you mean."

Paley didn't answer. He leaned against the edge of the desk. He found himself staring into the unfinished fireplace.

"Too bad it's not real," he said.

"Listen, Paley," she said. "I like you. And I really do appreciate everything you've done on this case. But something weird's been going on with you since the moment we met. You think I didn't see you staring at me in the mirror down in the lobby this morning? You think I can't read between the lines of what you're hinting at here?"

Paley felt himself blush.

"You forget," she said, smiling, "I'm an honorary Mental Midget now." Then she grew serious. "But I have a ten-year-old daughter, and that means something, you know? You want me, you want the child. I don't have time for games. If you're still interested, we'll see. If not, then let's be friends."

She held out her hand.

"Fair enough?" she said.

"Fair enough," Paley said, and he shook her hand.

They stayed that way for a moment, their hands holding, like two children tugging at a wishbone, each unwilling to be the first to let go.

But they did let go. Rose turned away. Paley pushed himself off the desk. He wanted to say something, to apologize, or to make a joke about how his girlfriend was always warning him that his flirting would get him in trouble one day. But he said nothing.

He looked away. So did Rose—into the fireplace. Then she turned toward the door.

"I hate to criticize," she called from the hallway, "but that poker is *fat*."

Chapter Six
THE DEAD

YES, the newspapers were right; snow was general all over Manhattan. Paley stood at the window in his living room, looking through the grillwork at the unseasonable fall of October snow. Snow made Jack Paley giddy, and always had. When he was little and snow fell during the week, he and his sister would huddle around the radio to find out if P.S. 41 was closed. If it was, Jack and Suze would go tearing around the apartment, shrieking and whooping until their mother told them that they weren't helping her headache one iota.

Today, he could have stood at the window for hours, wrapped in layers of sweatshirts, while the steam heat whistled and banged its way into his apartment. Fly-By-Night didn't have any work for Paley today; he might spend the morning at a museum, or at a series of SoHo galleries, or keep his promise to his artist friend Zack Taplinger to drop by his studio. Or he might stand here all morning, hands in pockets, just watching the snow. Only Belinda interrupted his reverie. "Paley," she said.

He turned and faced her. Belinda was standing beside the dresser holding a diaphragm case she had found in the drawer. She lifted it up in the air, almost victoriously, as though she had dug up the final item in a scavenger hunt. The tone of voice was not at all triumphant, however. "What's this?" she asked.

Paley was silent. "A clamshell I found on the beach?" he finally said.

"This isn't funny," said Belinda. "I'm really unhappy about this, you know."

"Whoa," he said. "What either of us did before we met each other is out of bounds."

"Before?"

"Of course, before. And nobody you know, anyway. *I* didn't even know that thing was still there, or I would have gotten rid of it."

"Oh," she said. "So it's not Rose's."

"Oh," he said. "Now I get it." Paley gripped Belinda gently by the shoulders; she was still wearing the football jersey she'd slept in, an outfit that always stirred him. It reminded him of the closing credits of "The Mary Tyler Moore Show;" the sight of a single woman in a football jersey capably soaping her car had provided Paley with a formative icon for the women's movement. "Look at me," he said, and he waited while Belinda raised her eyes. "The diaphragm case is definitely not Rose's. I am not having an affair with her, or with anybody."

"Well," she said, "even if it turns out you *were* having an affair with Rose, it would be none of my business."

"But I'm *not*," he said. "I'm not even *thinking* of having an affair with Rose."

"But you've been talking about her nonstop."

It was true. On Friday, the day after Sterling Ransom was arrested, Paley had dropped by the Eighth Precinct to find out the whole story. As Rose had told it, Ransom and Skinner had known each other well, but their business dealings in child pornography had gone sour and Skinner threatened to expose their mutual interest. Ransom resolved to kill him, so when Skinner called his apartment late at night and said they had to meet, it was an opportunity Ransom couldn't resist.

"You can't blame me," Paley said to Belinda now. "It's not every day I get to help out on a murder case. It's only natural I would want to talk about it, and Rose is part of that story. But my interest in her is purely professional."

He kissed Belinda on the cheek. "Okay?"

She shrugged. "Okay," she finally said.

But it was not okay. She tossed the diaphragm case into the back of the drawer, and she returned to rooting among his endless supply of socks, but he could see from the slope of her shoulders that she still wasn't convinced. Neither was Paley. Still, the irony of the situation wasn't lost on him; the one time he'd actually foresworn flirtation had turned out to be the one time Belinda suspected him of having an affair. It was some kind of cosmic justice, or joke, or both.

"Look," he said. He reached past Belinda now and plucked the object back out of the dresser drawer. While she watched, he walked it over to the kitchen and tossed it in the garbage. "There now," he said. "All gone. See?" He showed her his empty hands, turning them over.

Belinda smiled. "Okay, Paley, don't rub it in," she said, trying to keep her balance while pulling on a pair of bright-red, calf-length socks with a domino pattern that she'd found in his drawer. "I hope you don't mind if I borrow these. The weather caught me by surprise. It's the kind of day that makes you want to stay in bed."

She stood straight. "What do you think?"

"Those socks are *you*."

"That's not what I meant," said Belinda. "Want to play hooky? Fly-By-Night said they don't have any work today, right?"

He nodded his head.

"So?" she said.

"Any other time. Honest. But there's an errand I have to run today."

"Oh?"

"The Eighth Precinct."

"Oh."

"It's business," he said. "I have to see Rose about Herzog."

"What for?" she asked.

Paley explained that Herzog had called him a couple of times since their meeting at O'Shea's, and he had sounded more paranoid than ever. Paley had tried to calm him down, to assure him that the other Midgets were fine, but it hadn't been enough. Paley thought Rose might possibly pay a call on Herzog and make him feel better once and for all.

Belinda nodded her head.

"It's the truth," he said. "The guy's in trouble."

"I believe you."

"You've got to trust me."

"I do."

"After all," he said, "what's a relationship that's not based on trust?"

She shrugged. "Purely physical?"

Paley smiled. "We can play hooky for part of the day," he said, "if you want."

She turned toward him. A shudder ran over her.

"Can I leave my socks on?" she said.

Slowly he lifted her jersey.

The Eighth Precinct on a Wednesday morning was still showing the wear and tear of Tuesday night. A janitor walked around sweeping up the debris: whiskey bottles, loose change, an armless Cabbage Patch doll. A sudden shift in weather, Rose explained to Paley as she led him down a hall to her tiny office, makes the city jittery; enough people had been booked the night before to fill a soccer stadium.

"So what can I do for you?" she asked after sitting behind her desk, but the phone rang and she held up a hand. Paley settled himself carefully on a police-issue folding chair across from her and dutifully waited while she handled the call. It was like this the other time he'd visited Rose: a succession of interruptions. Even the momentary reprieves were charged with the certainty that any second now her name would be called down the hall, her phone would ring, her intercom would bleat. The deadened eyes in the WANTED posters on the wall, the laughter and muttered curses of suspects in the holding area, even the mountains of paperwork that never seemed to diminish: this environment could reduce a Zen master to tears. It all appealed to Paley, to his unsophisticated sense of cops-and-robbers; he'd even thought of asking Rose when the next police exam was. Paley was confident he could be a creditable cop, but he doubted he could handle the pressure as well as Rose. She seemed to flourish: a serene presence with keen, flashing eyes.

"My secret weapon," she'd told Paley the other day, when he'd asked how she did it, "is this." And she'd opened the center drawer of her desk, reached in, and pulled out a photo. "Even when I can't see it, I know it's in here," she said. "And there are times, plenty of times, every day, when I have to pull it out and remind myself of what's important and what's not."

She handed the photo to Paley. It was a snapshot of a girl in a Little League uniform.

"Tricia," said Rose.

"Wow," said Paley. Her forehead was high, just like her mother's, and her cheeks were high, too, but what gave the resemblance away was those eyes.

"You should get yourself one of these," Rose said, taking the photo back from Paley, studying it before she placed it back in her drawer. "Change your life."

Paley said that maybe he would, one day. Several times Rose had mentioned her daughter, had bragged about her accomplishments as a pitcher with the West Side Reds, and Paley had to admit to himself that he'd briefly toyed with the idea of what it would be like to marry Rose and automatically acquire a ten-year-old stepdaughter: It would be weird. But part of the thrill, he suspected, was knowing that he could have the cachet of fatherhood without any of the responsibilities. Besides, he and Rose were just friends, and it would stay that way.

Friendship, Paley was finding, was even safer than flirtation. When the two of them had sat around her office late into the evening last Friday, after the phones had stopped ringing but before the nightly round of arrests had started arriving, they'd traded stories of their pasts. Paley tried to describe what it was like to be a Mental Midget, to grow up with the burden of thinking that you and your friends are going to be the ones to change the world, and then to live with the knowledge that the world has somehow changed you. And Rose spoke of her past, of her own conviction that she and *her* friends would be the ones to change the world, of her own disappointments. But she also spoke of her own refusal to surrender to those disappointments, to believe that she'd failed. And then she'd pointed out the ancient SDS posters on the wall behind her desk. She kept them there as a reminder, she said, just like the photo of her daughter in the desk.

"Times change," she'd said. *"You* change. And you don't."

At the end of the evening Paley was grateful to be unencumbered by any of the usual awkwardnesses. He was free to say good-night to Rose without the pressure that comes from wondering about what happens next. Paley pedaled home that night, powered by an admiration, a respect—and maybe even a love—that for once felt pure.

"Toomey," Rose was explaining to Paley now, hanging up the phone. "Calling in sick. Thinks I don't know what's keeping him home is nothing but this snow. Well, that's all right. He'll have his pension soon enough, and he can spend it all on Ho Ho's and Yoo-hoo's, and I'll have a new partner. So," she said, sitting straighter, "where were we? Or is this visit just social?"

"Business," Paley said, eager to take advantage of Rose's undivided attention. "You know that old friend Davy Herzog I told you about?"

"The Midget," she said. "A loner."

"Right. Well, he's always been kind of a nut, but this time he's really panicking. Says someone tried to kill him. In his apartment. Says he's been living in fear ever since then. I've tried telling myself it's just some paranoid fantasy, but I just can't get it out of my mind."

"Well," said Rose, "I could send someone over." She reached for the telephone.

"No," said Paley. "I mean, as a favor to me, Rose, could you possibly go over yourself with me? Herzog needs to be treated with kid gloves. And by someone really willing to listen."

Rose paused. "Where did I get this reputation as someone *willing to listen?*" she said. "I'm a policewoman, not the leader of a rap session. This could damage my career." She looked at her watch and sighed.

"Well, maybe I can call this my lunch hour." She stood and pulled down a holster hanging from a hook and strapped it on. Then she grabbed the black police jacket draped across the back of her chair. "Let's go visit your friend the shut-in."

"Thanks so much," Paley said. "I don't know if I believe him, but I wouldn't bother you unless I thought it might be important."

"I know," she said. "For you, Paley, anything."

Paley shrugged, embarrassed. "Thrilled to hear it," he said.

Rose allowed herself a brief, broad smile before returning to her official posture: back straight, arms at her sides, eyes forward: those eyes again, deep and dangerous, the eyes of a markswoman, the eyes of a mother.

But Paley and Rose had barely begun their journey toward Herzog's address on lower Madison Avenue, their sedan cruising slowly over slippery streets, when her radio cried out for her attention. She spoke into the receiver, in an incantation of numbers and jargon that could only mean, Paley felt sure, their visit to Herzog would have to wait.

"A purse-snatching," Rose explained to Paley when she'd hung up. "Astor Place subway station. The MO seems to match a series of muggings in that area. Sorry, Paley, but I'm going to have to take a rain check on this thing with your wacky friend. Where can I drop you?"

"Rose," he asked, "is there any way I could come with you to the subway?"

She shook her head crisply. "No way; I'm not allowed to bring anyone along."

"I won't be conspicuous—promise."

"Regulations, Paley. You know better."

"Whatever happened to 'For you, anything'? Are we making exceptions already?"

"I don't know about you, but I certainly am," said Rose. "Now where can I drop you?"

"Well, you know, it just so happens I left my bike at home today, what with this snow and all. So I guess the best place to drop me would be—"

"—the Astor Place subway station, yeah, yeah." Rose sighed and made a sharp right turn.

The Astor Place subway station had undergone a transformation in recent years, changing from hellhole of the earth to a kind of subterranean Art Deco hangout for the young and hip. Indeed, many of the men and women standing on the platform were dressed in black and carrying portfolios of various sizes. Even the token seller wore a ruby stud in her nose.

Rose flashed her badge and the token seller nodded. Rose pushed open the gate, and Paley started to follow, but then he paused.

"Wait," he said. "There's something I've always wanted to do." He went back around to the fleet of turnstiles, chose one, and then jumped it, landing easily on the other side.

"Glad to see you're not being conspicuous," Rose muttered to him even as the officer already on the scene was waving her over. They nodded hello, and then he introduced the victim, Alison Sowecki. She was in her late twenties, and she wore half a scalp of bright-red hair. The other side of her head was shaved down to fuzz. She listened in silence while the earnest young officer repeated her description of the mugger: early twenties, male, and white—very white.

"Extremely blond," the victim spoke up. "Almost Nordic. But the weird part," she added, looking down the tracks, "is that he just seemed to disappear."

"Disappear?" Rose said.

"That's what got us thinking," said the officer, himself a blond. Paley leaned back against the subway wall, trying to look like someone waiting for a train.

"It's the identical MO we've been hearing about down here all week," the officer went on. "The attack takes place on Astor Place, only instead of running down the street the assailant runs into the subway station. By the time someone has a chance to follow, the mugger is gone. Nowhere. Not on the platform, and not outside the token booth. The token clerk here says she saw someone hop the turnstile, but that's nothing she doesn't see a hundred times a day. So there we have it: Wham, bam—and poof!"

Rose instructed the officer to take Ms. Sowecki over to the precinct; she said she'd handle matters underground. After the officer and the victim were gone, Rose turned to Paley and said, "This is good-bye, Paley."

"Say it ain't so."

Rose shook her head and started walking slowly along the platform, looking around. Paley tagged behind. A train trembled into the station, paused briefly, then trembled away. The smell of metal and urine lingered behind. Rose was oblivious of it all, jotting down notes in her pad. Paley had no idea what in the world she was writing: it might have been a shopping list, for all he knew, or an idea for a novel.

"You know," Rose finally spoke up, "I was talking to a transit cop friend of mine the other day about the subways. About how there are all these passageways in them." Rose squinted down the long, snaking tunnel with its slick tracks. "Maybe I should take a look."

"What would your partner, Toomey, do if he were here?" Paley said.

"Leave."

"Smart man."

She stepped onto the narrow catwalk that ran beside
the tracks, along the curved wall of the tunnel. Paley
followed; he couldn't help thinking how he could have
been back home with Belinda right now, playing hooky,
rolling around and giggling, staggering out of bed hours
later. But Paley let the fantasy recede and turned back
to the business at hand. Rose had no flashlight, but the
train signal lights on the tunnel walls provided illumina-
tion every few yards. The colors were beautiful: first
violet, then green, then red. Out of the corner of his
eye, Paley watched a rat slip by, its shiny fur glowing
red in the light. He shivered.

"Listen!" said Rose suddenly. She stopped walking
and Paley did, too. They stood on the narrow walkway
and listened to the distant sound. A rumble of men's
voices, with something higher and female cutting through.
"There are *people* here," said Rose.

"Maybe it's transit workers," Paley said.

"Maybe it's people who shouldn't be here," she said,
throwing him a significant look.

"I'm shocked, *shocked,*" Paley said in his best Claude
Rains, but already Rose had turned away.

Seconds later, another train rushed by them. Paley
felt a strong wind lift his hair, and the sound was so
loud he thought he would go deaf. The feeling was
nothing like the safe experience of standing calmly on a
platform; in the tunnel, a passing train meant tons of
steel pounding by only a few feet away. Sparks jumped
from rails. Lights flickered in the subway cars, and he
saw for a moment the faces of people on the train,
people reading newspapers or sleeping or straphanging,
none of them having any idea that someone *out there
in the darkness* was watching them. It was odd to
be in shadow; it was also a position of power. Paley
thought of the people he and Rose had heard up ahead.

They too must know the thrill of seeing but not being seen.

The train passed and all was quiet, except for the distant voices. Paley and Rose walked in silence, moving cautiously for a good ten minutes, until finally they found what they were looking for. The tunnel branched off to the right, and to the left there was a faint, orange light, and the locus of the distant voices, which now sounded quite close. Paley and Rose walked in the direction of the voices, and soon they found themselves in a startlingly cavernous space. The ceilings were high above; the floors were a mosaic of cement and earth. In the middle of this huge space, a small bonfire was burning; a group of people had sprawled around it on blankets and mats. Suddenly, one of the group turned his head.

"We've got company," he said.

Paley felt his heart jump. "Hello," he said, feigning a casual air. "We got a little lost." He almost made a joke, something stupid like, "We represent Mary Kay cosmetics. May we show you our new line of blush?" but intuitively stopped himself. People who lived below ground were probably not likely to be in a joking mood.

Rose said the word "Police" with quiet authority and flipped open her ID, as though anybody could possibly see it in this dim light.

Everyone just stared. From a distance the group looked benign, sitting around the fire as though enjoying a Boy Scout weenie roast. But no one here was telling ghost stories or singing "Kumbaya," and after a moment Paley began to see that something was disturbingly wrong with this picture. Although all the people around the fire were sitting or sprawling, they all looked ready to *spring* at any given moment. There was a potential for the unexpected here, Paley thought anxiously. He hung back and let Rose talk. He listened as she gently asked questions, trying to find out who these people were and how long they had been here.

No one was forthcoming. Answers were mumbled in monotones. They had been living here for weeks, one man explained. They weren't hurting anybody. They just liked it down here, where it was quiet. And indeed it was quiet down here; the only sound was the dripping of melted snow, which formed puddles on the ground, and the occasional roar of a faraway subway. From this distance the subway had an ethereal, almost beautiful sound; it could have been the roar of the ocean inside a seashell. Paley felt momentarily hypnotized. He was tired from all the walking, and he was cold; what he wanted to do was sit down beside the fire.

That was when he noticed the man. He was sitting between a thin woman and a younger, even thinner man, and his body was swathed in a blanket, but there was one startling feature about him: He was *albino*. Paley remembered that Alison Sowecki had described the purse snatcher as being *very* white. Paley turned toward Rose, but it was clear that she had long ago appraised the situation. She nodded almost imperceptibly at Paley, and he knew enough to be still.

"The thing is," she said to the group, "there have been some muggings in and around the subway lately, and we've got to check everyone in the area to see if they've seen anything."

"We told you," said the lone woman, "we haven't been out of here in weeks. This is where we hang out. The city is unlivable. Too expensive, too overdeveloped. We refuse to be a part of it. *This* is where we like to stay—underneath the nightmare, not in the middle of it."

"Hell is above us, not below," added the albino man.

Both of their voices had a strained, odd quality to

them, and Paley suddenly wondered if these people were addicts. He turned questioningly toward Rose, but once again, she gave him a look that let him know she was way ahead of him. Paley was embarrassed about his slow-wittedness, but actually, when it came to the latest designer drugs, he was quite ignorant. In boarding school and college, as if alcohol wasn't enough, he had smoked a lion's share of powerful dope and had once chewed psilocybin mushrooms with a girl named Cindy from his Virginia Woolf seminar, but that was about as far as it went. In more recent years, lucidity had become a priceless and sometimes fleeting thing for Paley. He worked so much and thought so hard that he often found his vision blurring over of its own accord.

When Paley really looked at these people now, he saw that they seemed both stoned and agitated. "I know you say that you haven't been out of here in weeks," said Rose, "but I'm curious about how you manage with food and all."

"We don't have to answer anything," said a dark-haired man with narrow eyes, and murmurs of agreement came from around the circle.

"I'll tell you how we manage," said the albino, his voice cutting through the others. Everyone else was silent. "In fact," he went on, "I'll even show you."

He stood up shakily, dusting off his knees and letting the blanket fall to the ground. The whiteness of his skin and hair, combined with the pale light to his eyes, gave him a startlingly lupine look. His ripped jeans stopped several inches short of his ankles; he was almost as tall as Paley, but he walked with a severe stoop, as if he were carrying upon his shoulders the weight of the city above. Paley and Rose followed him into the recesses of the cavernous space. In one dim corner he showed them a larder of soup cans. In another there was an impro-

vised toilet, with an impressive supply of toilet paper
stacked in a pyramid nearby. And in a third corner, he
showed them a row of bedrolls. There were also kero-
sene lamps and paperback books. These people had
really made a life for themselves down here, and Paley
had to admit he was impressed. He even said so.

The man regarded Paley in the dim light.

"Gabriel," the man said after a pause. "My name's
Gabriel." Then he smiled grimly. "I know I haven't
created Utopia, but it's a step. Do you understand?"

His voice was slow, determined.

"Yes," Paley said. "I understand."

"I believe you do," Gabriel said. "You look like an
honest man. I myself am an honest man. We are, all of
us down here, honest. But the world is not. We tried
living up there, we played by the rules, and do you
know what? They don't work. That's why we're *here*."
He brought his foot down. "Every day up there we
would witness acts of unspeakable cruelty and greed,
examples of violence against man, woman, and child,
and we would try to tell ourselves that after enough
time we would get used to it, that we could learn to live
with this. But we couldn't. Nobody can. And now the
world is paying for the excesses of humanity. The very
planet is in revolt. Earthquakes, plagues, and the ice
caps are shifting. Each summer is hotter than the last,
yet snow falls in October." He gestured toward the
incessant dripping from the ceiling. "It's better down
here," he said. "Hard to believe, I know. But I've seen
the world from both sides, and I tell you, it's better
down here." And then he fell silent.

Paley fantasized for a moment about living in this
world, giving in to the anarchistic tendencies that had
been brought out in him in college, only to scuttle back
inside quickly when he graduated. Almost everyone was
a four-year anarchist, Paley thought. He was. Rose was.

Very few people stayed with the cause beyond graduation day.

Suddenly a squawk emanated from Rose's walkie-talkie. "I have to take this," she said, and she spoke some cryptic words into the receiver. She listened for a moment then turned her back on Paley and Gabriel and walked a few yards away to continue her conversation in private. When she came back, she seemed different.

"Paley," she said, returning her walkie-talkie to its place on her hip, "that friend of yours, that Herzog character. The one who lives in the office building. What's his name?"

"Herzog," said Paley. "You just said it."

"*First* name," said Rose.

Paley was puzzled. "Davy," he said. "Why?"

Rose winced. "I just got a call in on him," she said. "Amazing but true. They told me I should go to the same address on Madison you and I were just heading to. An office building. Apartment Four-D." She paused. "Suicide," she said.

A flood of acid rose in Paley's throat. "I'm going to be sick," he said, and he clapped his hand over his mouth.

"Steady," said Rose, and she put an arm around him. Paley leaned against her, breathing deeply, collecting himself, trying not to puke. Not puking, Paley had always thought, was one of the great advantages of giving up drinking. It had been years since he'd spent a morning folded into a fetal position on the tiles before a toilet, but the memory returned to him now in a rush. Of all the activities available to humans, puking was the worst. After a moment, he felt a little better, and the swell of nausea was replaced by a swell of *truth*. Herzog had been right, he had been right all along, and Paley hadn't acted quickly enough. It was terrible; it couldn't be worse.

"How?" Paley said in a tiny, strained voice. "How did he do it?"

"Jumped," said Rose.

"He didn't. He wouldn't."

"Let's get out of here," Rose said. "I've got to get over to Herzog's building, and I want to get you above ground. I'm sure you're not interested in subway life anymore." She turned to address Gabriel. "And as for *you*," she said, "I have no warrant to search any of you, but I guarantee that the cops who come back are going to have one. And if they find drugs, then you're all going to be busted. For the moment, all I'm investigating is a few purse-snatchings, so I don't really have anything further to say to you today. But be warned."

She quickly said good-bye to the campfire crowd and turned back toward the tunnel.

"Rose," Paley whispered a couple of steps behind her, "shouldn't we stay here until we finish?"

"What's to finish?"

"I don't know. These people—"

"Look, right now I've got a suicide to take care of."

"But that man, that Gabriel—"

She shook her head. "I know what you're going to say," she said. "You're going to say that the man's an albino, and our suspect is described as *very* fair haired. But that's not enough to go on. In the sixties," she continued, her voice growing impassioned, "when Angela Davis was wanted by the FBI, cops used to routinely bring in black girls with big Afros who were just walking down the street minding their own business. It happened to *me*. And I will not be a part of that kind of thing, Paley. I can't bring in every blond person I see. And besides," she added, "I believe those people. They may be strange and drugged out and all, but I guess I have a soft spot for political conviction. They've got everything they need down here: food, shelter, books, probably drugs, sure, but they seem . . . I don't know . . . *committed.*"

They were heading along the snaking tracks. Paley thought about Herzog, dead in his apartment. He wondered if death was like a subway tunnel: endless, dark, deep beneath the earth, almost unreachable. The difference, he supposed, was that up ahead in the subway tunnel, Paley could see a green signal light. Civilization. Signs of life.

"Rose," Paley said softly, touching her shoulder. She turned around.

"What?"

"Maybe you should go back to the campfire and bring Gabriel in for questioning."

"I just *told* you."

"I know," Paley continued. "But you've *got* a reasonable suspicion, Rose. If you gave it a little thought now, you'd see what I mean."

The Extra Credit Question is:

What *Did* Paley Mean?

(Solution on next page)

∫olution

"Gabriel made a crucial mistake," Paley said.

"Mistake?" Rose said.

"I almost believed what he was saying, about how much he hates violence and injustice, and to his mind it's probably all true," Paley said. "But this guy's also a survivor. He knows what he has to do. And if that includes making periodic excursions up to Astor Place and grabbing a purse, so be it. He may hate the world up there, but he visits it, all right. Regularly. Not weeks ago, like he said. But today."

"How can you be sure?" she said.

"Because he referred to the freak October snowstorm we're having. He even pointed to it." Paley pointed now, up at the dripping from the ceiling. "That's melted snow, all right, but by the time it gets down here it *looks like rain*."

"So the only way he would know it was snowing today, and not raining," Rose said, "is if he saw it for himself."

She unclipped the walkie-talkie from her hip and called for a few more cops to be sent over immediately. Then she turned to Paley and insisted that he leave.

"No," he said, "I have to go with you. To Herzog's."

"Not this time. I won't allow it."

"But what about 'For you, anything'?"

"This *is* for you," she said. "I want you out of here. Out of subway tunnels and suicides and the rest of the shit that Rommel was right about."

She leaned over and Paley felt her breath in his ear.

"Go home," she whispered.

And so Paley did. Rose knew best. He caught a downtown train, then walked quickly through SoHo, skidding along the slick sidewalks. His nausea had passed; in its place was fatigue—an overwhelming drowsiness, an urge to drop right here, right now, a chill that seemed to be settling in for the long haul. Back at his building, Mrs. Cellini wanted to know something about the route taken by Sir Francis Drake, but Paley couldn't answer. He couldn't even understand the question. Rose knew best. He had to go home.

Yes, the newspapers were right; snow was general all over Manhattan. His soul swooned slowly as he heard the snow falling faintly through the universe and faintly falling, like the descent of their last end, upon all the living and the dead.

Chapter Seven
FLOATING ISLAND

THIS time, there was no memorial service. Herzog's family, who lived in Florida, wanted to do their grieving in private. And Herzog had very few friends; his paranoia had been too restrictive to allow many confidants into his life. Still, the Saturday after Herzog's death, Paley stayed in bed. He didn't want to do anything today, didn't want to read the papers or go shopping or eat brunch at one of SoHo's many bruncheries. This was not a day for a salmon-and-leek omelet accompanied by a hired quartet of Juilliard students playing Vivaldi. This was a day for mourning.

The truth could not be avoided: He might have been able to help Herzog, if only he had begun to believe his story earlier. Paley lay in bed alone, wearing a pair of boxer shorts with tiny blue crescent moons on them, a present from Belinda. He smoked a cigarette and looked out the window at the bright day. His telephone rang and rang and he let the machine pick up the call. It was Belinda, big surprise, wanting to know what was going on, why he hadn't called her in more than a day. "Are you okay, honey?" she asked. Then there was a long sigh. "Check in soon so I know *you're* not dead, too," she said, and then she signed off.

Paley thought about calling her right back, telling her he felt lousy and asking if she might consider coming over. But then he realized he didn't want to be pampered, and in a way he thought it might be better to be left alone. He felt like an old dog who slinks off into a corner to die. And perhaps that was what he was doing. After all, both Larry Kelleher and Herzog had died in their own homes. Paley felt uneasy about this fact, but his sadness was stronger than his fear, and so he kept lying there in his loft bed, feeling vaguely vulnerable to attack but not really working up the impetus to move. He lay there as the light changed in the room and the afternoon settled in. The telephone rang again; this time it was his mother.

"Paley," she said, "you never call anymore. You never let us know how you're doing." She sighed a heavy, boozy sigh. "I remember when you and Suze were little, you were so affectionate. You'd come up to me in the morning with big smiles on your faces. . . ." Her voice broke off. "Well, I don't want to be a thorn around your neck, but I just wanted to tell you we missed you and would love to have you to dinner anytime. You can bring that nice Smith girl, too. Not that 'performance artist' you brought home once."

His mother meant Nova, née Lisa Berger, whom he had brought with him to Thanksgiving a few years before, and had yet to hear the end of. How Nova had cried when Paley's father sliced the turkey. How Nova had cried at the Macy's parade when the Bullwinkle blimp floated by. A sentimental girl, that Nova. But then his parents met Belinda and fell in love with her. Paley's mother always referred to Belinda as "that nice Smith girl" even though Belinda had gone to an alternative college somewhere in Oregon. But she *looked* like a Smith girl, and that was good enough for Paley's alcoholic mother. Paley listened to his mother's monologue now, but he certainly didn't have the desire to call her back. He didn't have the desire to call anyone, not even Belinda. Paley continued to lie in his bed. At some point, his buzzer sounded, and he forced himself to answer the door.

It was Belinda, bearing gifts. In the history of their relationship, this was the first time she had ever shown up unannounced.

"Smoked Gouda," she said, unpacking a bag of high-priced groceries from Dean & DeLuca. "Tricolored vegetable terrine. Raspberry tartlet."

Paley thanked her and put the items in his refrigerator, next to a half-empty container of plain yogurt (or was it half full? his freshman Buddhist Thought professor would have asked), an old prescription bottle of ear drops, and a bunch of trod-upon-looking dill.

"What are you doing, trying to clinch the Most Pathetic Refrigerator Contents award?" Belinda asked. Paley stood in front of the draft from the open refrigerator door, and just then the small light bulb inside blew out with a tiny pop. "The winner!" said Belinda.

Paley closed the door and leaned against it. "I'm really down. I just can't seem to shake it."

She stood beside him and stroked his hair. "I know," she said softly. "Come home with me today. Spend the night with me tonight. I know it isn't Tuesday, but you shouldn't be alone. You're a mess, Paley. Come on; come home with me. It won't kill you."

Paley looked at her. The phrase ran through him like a long, slow electric charge. "I'm not so sure of what might or might not kill me anymore," he said. "Look at Herzog. Look what happened to him." He shook his head. "You can't understand."

"Paley," said Belinda, and she sighed deeply. "It's terrible what happened to Herzog. *Terrible*. And I want to understand what you're feeling, but you just shut me out sometimes. I know I'm not a genius, and I know I wasn't a Mental Midget, but maybe I can help you. Maybe I can be of some use.''

Paley kissed Belinda very gently on the mouth. Then he pulled back and said, ''You're terrific, Belinda. You're smart and loving and you bring me smoked Gouda and vegetable terrine that looks like the Italian flag. And I'm more grateful than you know. But today''—and here Paley looked out the window, across the rooftops of a city that was full of both wonderful and deadly surprises—''today, I think you should go home.''

''Okay,'' said Belinda, ''I'll—''

''Alone.''

Belinda retreated reluctantly, and Paley returned to bed. He played with a Slinky, he smoked cigarettes, he watched the Home Shopping Network. Outside the window, the New York sky darkened slowly.

At eight that evening, the telephone rang and a woman with a British accent began to speak into the machine. ''Hallo there, Jack Paley,'' she began. ''This is a *blahst* from your recent *pahst.*'' The voice sounded familiar, but the only women who came to mind were Julie Andrews and Hayley Mills. Paley sat up in bed and began to listen with interest. *Andie Sparrow; that's who it was.* He had not spoken to the actress since his last day of work on *Women Who Love Too Much: The Musical.* Since then, the show had opened and closed with amazing alacrity and with an amazing lack of fanfare. The only redeeming element of the musical, according to the drama critic of the *Times,* had been the shining presence of Andie Sparrow.

''Remember me?'' she asked after Paley picked up the phone and announced that he was home.

''Of course I remember you,'' he said. ''You're the only woman who's ever heard my Katharine Hepburn impression.''

Andie laughed. "I'm honored to have that distinction," she said. "Maybe if I play my cards right, I'll hear your Carole Lombard, too." She paused. "Look, do you remember a certain conversation we had, once upon a time?" she asked. "In which you promised to go out on the town with me should I ever happen to ask you?"

"Yes."

"Well, I happen to be asking you now. There's a party tonight."

"Tonight?" Paley groaned. He was certainly in no shape to paint the town red with Andie Sparrow; he could barely get out of bed. But she kept talking and he began to reconsider; perhaps it would do him a world of good to get out of bed and out of his apartment. To spend the evening with someone he barely knew but certainly liked, someone with whom he could have a little fun. Someone to whom he wouldn't have to explain himself. With Belinda, he would have had to pour his heart out, but Andie knew nothing about his problems. The idea of an evening with Andie Sparrow began to appeal to him. "Sure," he said finally. "I'd love to go."

"It's not a death sentence," said Andie. "There are some men in this city who would die to get a date with me. You know, I was even first prize in *Rockworld* magazine one month. The winner got to ride around the park in a limo with me, drinking champagne. His name was Neil and he was a high school sophomore. What a thrill. In fact, it's *Rockworld* that's throwing this party. Their annual bash."

So Paley finally agreed to meet her at eleven at the entry of a new nightclub called The Steerage Bar. Open only a month, it was currently the most desirable club in Manhattan. Or rather, *near* Manhattan. The Steerage Bar was actually located on Ellis Island, once the city's immigration entry point. For a while there had been a museum on Ellis Island, but when that proved not lucrative enough for the city, an entrepreneur got the clever idea to turn this place—which had long ago served as the landing station for the weary and hopeful—into the landing station for the fashion-conscious and androgynous.

Paley stepped into a bath, ran soap over all the important parts, then rinsed and dried off. When he was done, he pulled his good linen suit out of the closet and yanked a pretty blue tie off the rack. His fingers formed a quick knot; he had worn ties so many times in his life that he could make knots in his sleep. Then he stood before the full-length mirror and examined himself. Not too bad for a man who had been lying in bed all day thinking morbid thoughts. For someone so depressed, Paley looked rather festive.

At ten-forty, Paley boarded the Ellis Island ferry. The trip was brief and calm; after Wednesday's unseasonal snowstorm, autumn had returned, so Paley sat outside, smoking by the rail. Andie was waiting for him when he disembarked.

"Right on time," she said, kissing his cheek. She took him by the arm and led him toward the huge building. The entrance to the club was mobbed. Lording over the crowds were two strapping bouncers dressed as turn-of-the-century immigration officials, holding lengthy lists of whom to let in and whom to turn away. A couple of photographers who had been leaning against the chain-link fence now snapped to life, descending on Andie and her unknown escort. Paley tried to step out of the frame, but she drew him back in. Little did he know that the caption in the next day's *Post* would read, "Andie Sparrow and her not-so-secret admirer."

"Come on," she whispered, "don't you want your fifteen minutes?"

"I think I used them up before puberty," he said. She

looked at him blankly, but he didn't have time to explain.

Paley stood there, grinning and going blind from the persistent flashes. So much for the Ellis Island motif, he thought as a chorus of cameras whirred and clicked. He tried to imagine this same scene taking place eighty years before: Essie and Sol Moskowitz arriving from Minsk, blinded by flashbulbs, saying, "Please, boys, no pictures!"

Suddenly one of the bouncers grabbed Andie and Paley by their arms and pulled them through the crowd. Then something cold and wet was slapped down on the back of Paley's left hand. It took him a moment to realize that he and Andie had been stamped with invisible markings; Paley felt slightly ashamed at his sudden emergence from the tide of would-be club guests to the ranks of the elect.

Paley and Andie walked into a dark, glittering main room where sound exploded and videos were projected on giant screens overhead. On one screen, a German Shepherd licked a woman from head to toe; on another, Siamese twins played checkers. Was Diane Arbus directing music videos from beyond the grave? The music in the club was a mixture of New Wave and old standards from Paley's college days. He remembered being eighteen and playing woozy air guitar to these songs, standing in his dorm room in Adams House wearing cutoffs and a flannel shirt, his hands crawling along the neck of some imaginary stringed instrument. Now he was dressed to the nines and squiring a three-time Grammy winner to a party at one of the most sophisto clubs in town. Paley decided that he had come a long way since college. A couple of women in black pillbox hats walked by and sized him up, and then one of them smiled openly at him. Paley smiled back awkwardly, then turned away. It was strange the way he seemed to

belong here, just because his hair hung in his face a
certain way and he had on a good-looking, baggy suit
and his arm was linked through Andie Sparrow's. But
he realized, looking around this huge, dark room with
its pockets of humanity and inhumanity, its glow of
cigarette tips and chatter of ice in glasses, that tonight
he didn't feel even remotely comfortable in this world.
Unlike most of these people, Paley couldn't just arrive
at a club and leave his cares with the hatcheck-cum-
immigration girl. He brought them inside; he carried
them with him onto the dance floor, over to the open
bar where he stared wistfully at men and women drinking gin martinis and scotches on the rocks, and upstairs
to the VIP lounge, where Andie dragged him after they'd
been dancing for all of five minutes.

"I should put in an appearance," she said. "I mean,
this is where Dexter Flamm—you know, the editor in
chief—plants himself for the whole night. He doesn't
like to be disturbed by the riffraff at these parties,
especially if they've got nothing to do with the music
business."

"The great unwashed," Paley said. "The great tone
deaf."

"You've got it. With Dexter either you're a star or
you're a nobody."

"So here we go," said Paley. "The star and the
nobody."

"Not quite. You're a star to me. And if Dexter Flamm
acts snotty, we'll just leave." She smiled. "He can't
afford to alienate me—he wants me for the June cover."

The VIP lounge was guarded by two more bouncers.
Now, even among the privileged few whose presences
had been requested at the Steerage Bar tonight, a further division was occurring. Outside the VIP room a
group had gathered: the assistant editors, the publicists,
the record company junior execs, the sound engineers,

all of them sipping their drinks with drop-dead nonchalance and sneaking hungry peeks inside the VIP lounge, where the music industry's nucleus of power had gathered for the night. As it turned out, Paley was almost forced to wait outside the lounge while Andie went inside and paid her respects.

"Your friend's not on the list," one of the two bouncers told Andie in a flat voice after she gave both of their names.

"He's with me," Andie said.

"I can see that, Miss Sparrow," the bouncer said, "but tonight we're under orders from Mr. Flamm that nobody gets in the VIP lounge unless they're on the VIP list."

"I guess I'm just not VI enough," Paley said, but Andie wasn't listening.

"Can't you make an exception?" she said.

"It's all right, Andie," Paley said. "I don't mind. I'd almost prefer it. This is getting embarrassing."

"It's not all right," she said, turning to him. "It's my own fault. I should have remembered to have them put you on the list." Suddenly her face brightened. "Of course," she said to the bouncer, "if one of you would care to ask Mr. Flamm yourself . . ."

The two bouncers looked at each other but already seemed resigned to their fate: One of them would have to pay the testy host of the party a personal visit. While the bigger of the two slouched off to talk to Flamm, Paley wondered how many more levels of elitism there could possibly be within one nightclub. It was almost as elaborate as Dante's many-layered Hell.

In a moment the bouncer sullenly returned to report that Dexter Flamm would be delighted to welcome any friend of Andie's into the inner sanctum. Then, sighing deeply, he pushed open the door to let them pass. The air inside the lounge seemed at least five degrees cooler, and the music was much softer. The room, Paley realized, looked like a suburban living room circa 1965. Men and women, most of them famous, sat around on sofas and La-Z-Boys beneath ugly oil paintings and sunburst clocks. In a corner, leaning back into the aqua cushions of a low sectional couch that wouldn't have been out of place in the home of Rob and Laura Petrie, peering out from under a Brooklyn Dodgers baseball cap and receiving his visitors with barely a nod of his head, slouched Dexter Flamm. At twenty-nine, exactly Paley's age, the man was famous for being editor in chief of one of the most successful rock magazines ever. But he was also famous for being a world-class brat, for making scenes at editorial board meetings, for shoveling up hills of cocaine while an art director was patiently trying to show him the boards for the next issue.

"Andie," Dexter said when she approached. He tilted up the visor of his hat so that his small eyes were revealed. Paley couldn't help but think of a lab rat that had been fed too many drugs through a dropper.

"This is my good friend Jack Paley," said Andie.

"Paley, Paley," said Flamm, mulling it over. He squinted. "You once play drums with the Patti Smith Group?" Paley shook his head. "Bass with the Pretenders?" He shook his head again. "Guitar with REO Speedwagon?" Paley shook his head. "You ever have a baby out of wedlock with Whitney Houston?" Paley started to shake his head once more, but Dexter Flamm had already lost interest. What was interesting him, apparently, was the fact that his glass was empty. He waved his empty tumbler vaguely, and at once a waiter materialized to refill it.

Andie poked Paley with her elbow, and he took this as their cue to retreat. "Now we can dance," Andie said, and she showed Paley the smile that had graced the covers of all her albums—only this time her teeth glowed purple in the dark. It took him a moment to realize why: They had moved into a section of the VIP lounge that was illuminated by ultraviolet light. Paley looked down at his linen suit, and it, too, glowed, though not as brightly as the sliver of white shirt that poked out from the end of his sleeve.

"What are you looking at?" Andie asked, and Paley flashed her a wide smile. Andie looked from his smile down to her own skintight, sequined minidress, then back at him. She laughed, and in that moment Paley put his problems into perspective. Maybe he couldn't escape his depression by coming to a trendy nightclub. Maybe he wouldn't be able to figure out why two of his old friends had died. Maybe he couldn't even pick a career, any career, and get on with his life. But at the moment what Paley knew for sure is that there were worse fates in life than squiring a beautiful young icon to a nightclub.

And it was more than her laugh: What really endeared Andie to him was the way she raised her hand to her face, as if to cover her mouth. On the back of her hand, the X that had been stamped there at the door glittered like a jewel. Here she was, that most public of figures, a pop music star, yet she could still be embarrassed by something as simple as purple teeth. Another celebrity might not have been so shy—and as if to offer that contrast, it was precisely at this moment that Paley noticed Dexter Flamm. The editor was still seated on his couch, but now he was heatedly waving something at one of the bouncers. Paley assumed it was an empty glass, but then Dexter's hand stopped slicing through the air just long enough for Paley to see that it was an audio cassette. Paley and Andie exchanged raised eyebrows and giggled, then inched themselves across the dance floor until they were wriggling within eavesdropping distance.

"This is unbelievable," Flamm was muttering. "This is just unbelievable."

"What's the problem?" the bouncer said.

"The problem?" said Dexter Flamm. "The problem is that somebody here doesn't know how to do his job."

The bouncer paused, nodded, then reached inside his jacket and produced a walkie-talkie. "Trouble in VIP city," he said into the receiver.

"It's too late," Flamm went on. "You can't assuage me. My privacy has been violated and no apology is going to bring it back. I mean, what's the point of a VIP room if just anyone can get in and slip me an audition tape?"

"Come on," Paley whispered to Andie. "We don't need this."

He tried to lead her by the elbow, past the VIPs, far out of the reach of Flamm's voice. But Paley succeeded in moving Andie only out of the pool of ultraviolet light.

"What's this?" she said. "My favorite detective has lost his curiosity?" Paley shrugged. Andie tilted her head as if to study him. "What's wrong?" she asked more softly. "You can tell me. All night long you've had something on your mind." She took a step toward Paley. The same hand that had shyly covered her purple smile now touched his face.

Paley shrugged. She was right, of course: It wasn't like him to walk away from a situation that he didn't fully comprehend. But then, it wasn't like him to walk away from the death of a friend, which is what he'd done these past two days. Still, what was the use in involving her in his troubles? He and Andie had somehow wound up near the bar, and Paley watched as a female bartender in a red uniform with brass buttons shook a jigger and poured a drink. An eager hand found its way around the glass, and the bartender was on to her next order. All these people could just drink the night away and let their problems spontaneously combust. The realization almost made Paley tremble. He imagined putting a glass to his lips and taking a swallow of gin as cold as water from a stream. The memory of the taste was overpowering, and it led to other thoughts. He imagined poor Herzog tumbling from his window, and he was both sickened and heartsick from the thought. A drink would unmoor such thoughts, would pull him away and onto some floating island where he could spend the night dancing and forgetting.

"What'll it be?" a woman's voice asked, and Paley found himself staring closely into the face of the bartender.

"A gin martini," he said weakly, amazed that he was hearing himself say the words. He half-expected the bartender to look at him in shock and say, "Hey, bub, you know you can't drink! You took a vow, you completed a twelve-step program!" But instead she barely nodded, then grabbed hold of a big, clear bottle with a metal nozzle, and commenced to pour.

"Paley," said Andie, "talk to me."

In a moment his hand was wrapped around the martini. He felt the skin above his upper lip start to sweat. "I can't," he said.

"Then dance with me," said Andie. And she innocently took the glass from his hand, placed it on an empty table, and led him into a dark corner of the lounge. In her high heels, she was able to perch her head on his shoulder lightly, companionably. And in a few moments he had begun to relax, and when she whispered, still swaying to the music, "What gives?" he found himself almost wanting to talk.

"It's this friend—" Paley began, but then he stopped himself. Was it accurate to describe Herzog as a friend? Is that really what Herzog had been to him, and he to Herzog? A real *friend* would have listened to Herzog's warnings. A real friend would have tried to do something . . . instead of mooning around his apartment all day, or even going out to a nightclub with a pop star. The more Paley thought about it, the worse he felt, but still he struggled to talk about it. "This *acquaintance,* he—" Paley tried, and then he had to stop himself again. None of the words that presented themselves seemed adequate: "died," "passed away," "expired" —what could do justice to what had happened to Herzog?

And what *had* happened to Herzog, anyway? Three days after his death, the details still remained unclear to Paley. A true friend—even an acquaintance with a conscience—would have looked into the matter by now. So why hadn't Paley done exactly that? Why had he interpreted Herzog's death only as a reminder of his own mortality, instead of investigating the possibility that Herzog's conspiracy plans weren't simply the product of a paranoid mind? Would it have killed Paley to give Herzog the benefit of the doubt one last time?

But that was it: What if it *would* kill Paley? What if Herzog was right—that the odds against two household deaths among a small circle of friends within a couple of weeks of each other were too astronomical to ignore? Is that what Paley was really afraid of? Before he had a chance to consider this question—or for that matter, any of Andie's questions—Paley was pulled away from these thoughts by the rising voice of Dexter Flamm.

"This is what I'm talking about, Millicent," he was saying. "This is what's ruining my evening."

Millicent, the entrepreneur who owned The Steerage Bar but who made more appearances in New York gossip columns than on the premises of her own club, stood with her hands on her hips in front of the angry editor. She was a small bottle-blonde with spit curls and fur-trimmed clothing. Except for the fur, she looked like someone who might wait tables at a bowling alley.

Millicent nodded to a bouncer, who took the cassette from Flamm's hand and opened the plastic case.

"There's a note," he said, pulling a card from the case.

Paley leaned closer to listen.

The bouncer cleared his throat. " 'Dear Mr. Flamm,' " he began. " 'Everyone says that you are always looking to discover new musical talent. My friends and I have a band called Barbie's Dream House, and we think we deserve a listen. We don't expect to be on the cover of *Rockworld,* but maybe a mention could help us get started.' "

"Is that it?" said Millicent.

"Just a signature," said the bouncer. "Looks like Adam Spock or something. And then a phone number." He sniffed. "The area code is Queens or Brooklyn or Staten Island," he added with disdain.

Millicent, who originally hailed from Flatbush, a neighborhood in Brooklyn, turned to Flamm. "I'm truly sorry," she said, "that your privacy has been disturbed. But it simply seems like some pathetic Battle of the Bands teenager looking for a break."

"Listen," Flamm said, "it's bad enough I'm forced to include stories in the magazine on so-called 'new talent,' which basically means kids who weren't even born when the Beatles broke up. But when I'm not at the office, I don't want to deal with this kind of garbage." He swiveled his gaze toward the bouncer. "I thought his job was to keep the uninvited out of the VIP lounge."

"Dexter," Millicent said, putting a hand on his shoulder, "I do apologize for the inconvenience, but the night is young, and you and your friends can still salvage the evening."

But this wasn't enough for Flamm. "Obviously somebody screwed up," he continued. "I know everybody in this so-called VIP lounge of yours, and there's no Adam Spock here."

"I'm sure you're right," said Millicent. She was starting to get bored with the conversation, and her gaze was drifting across the lounge, to where a Woodstock legend was cleaning his teeth with a minted toothpick.

"Obviously someone got past your guards here and snuck this note to me and then got out," Flamm persisted. "Why should I hold my annual *Rockworld* blowout here if you're not going to give me adequate protection? Jesus, any other club in this town would go into convulsions of happiness if I decided to throw next year's party chez them: Beasley's, The Sperm Bank, Hanna-Barbera's . . ."

"Now hang on there," said the bouncer. He jerked a thumb over his shoulder at the other bouncer, still on duty at the door to the lounge. "Nobody who's not on the VIP list gets past me and my cobouncer." He paused, then added in a quiet, proud voice, "We worked for *Stallone* for three months."

"They should take away your bouncer's license," muttered Flamm.

"Now wait a minute, Mr. Flamm," Paley heard himself pipe up from the corner where he and Andie stood. Despite his anxiety, his voice came out with surprising power.

Millicent swiveled toward him. "And who," she pronounced flatly, "is this?"

Paley gave her his name and then kept talking before she had a chance to ask him if he had played slide guitar with the Boomtown Rats. It was either going to be a moment of deep embarrassment or deep triumph. He looked at Andie to see if she was shrinking away from him, but instead she had her arms folded and was watching him keenly, expectantly.

"What I have to say," Paley went on, "is this: Suppose the bouncers were doing a terrific job. Suppose the person who got past them was somebody who was *supposed* to get past them. Like another employee."

"Impossible," said Millicent, turning away from him. "I take pride in closely monitoring every aspect of my various enterprises, and I can assure you that the name of Adam Kirk does not appear on any payroll of mine."

"That's Spock," said Paley.

"Whatever," said Millicent. "There is no one of that name in my employ. Nor was there anyone of that name on the VIP list tonight. I went over that list myself. And," she continued, "there wasn't even anyone of that name on the guest list at the door *downstairs* tonight."

"But I wasn't on any list either," said Paley. "Andie was. What I mean is, just because someone wasn't invited doesn't mean he couldn't get past the front door as the guest of someone else who *was* invited. And once he gets past the front door, what's to stop him from seeing the famous young editor Dexter Flamm—except that he hasn't counted on the fact Flamm has secluded himself inside the VIP lounge?"

"So you're saying I did screw up," said the bouncer.

"Not at all," said Paley. "Look," he continued, "let's try an experiment."

"Let's not," said Millicent.

"It'll take five minutes," said Paley. Both Millicent and Flamm looked at him coldly, but he persevered. "How many waiters are working the club tonight?" he said.

Flamm looked to Millicent, and Millicent started to open her mouth in protest. But then she sighed, closed her eyes, and said, "Nine."

"Good," said Paley. "Now all you have to do is arrange for every waiter in the club to stop by the lounge, one at a time, and ask Andie Sparrow if there's anything she needs."

"That's it?" said Millicent.

"That's it," Paley said. "We'll be waiting over there," he said, and before Millicent had a chance to object, he led Andie over to a green Naugahyde La-Z-Boy in the corner.

"Well, you're certainly not a *boring* date," Andie observed as she settled into the chair. "Depressed, maybe. Boring, no." She paused, remembering something. "Before we got sidetracked by this little VIP-lounge saga," she said, "you were starting to say something about your friend."

"He died," Paley said. "He was an acquaintance, really, and he died. He was the second acquaintance of mine to die in the last few weeks."

"That's rotten," said Andie softly. "I've seen some of that myself lately—so many of my theater friends in London. It's hard, I know it is. Everyone is losing someone to this plague." She took his hand.

"It wasn't AIDS." Paley paused. "It was . . . violence."

Andie's eyes widened momentarily. "That's awful."

He opened his mouth to speak when a small, affable waiter appeared at their side and asked Andie if she needed anything.

Paley studied him, then shook his head slightly. "No," Andie said, "but thanks." The waiter retreated.

"You were starting to say something, Paley?" Andie asked.

Paley nodded. "The thing is, this second acquaintance told me just days before he died that he thought someone was trying to kill him. And I didn't listen."

"You can't blame yourself."

"You have no idea how much I can blame myself."

"Miss Sparrow, can I get you anything?" asked another waiter, this one tall and thin. Again, Paley studied him and shook his head. Andie said, "No, thanks."

After the waiter was gone, Paley unburdened himself. He told Andie all about "The Mental Midgets." He told her about Herzog, his paranoia, his conspiracy theory, his unlikely death—or at least Paley told her as much as he knew. "The rest," he said, "is a mystery. Exactly how he died. And why."

Andie looked at him. "I'm sorry about your friend, I really am," she began, but he interrupted her.

"Acquaintance," he corrected.

"*Friend*," Andie insisted. "You went out for drinks with him a few days before his death, and a few days after his death you're still not satisfied with the official explanations. In fact, it's eating you alive. That," she said, "is friendship."

"Do you need anything, Miss Sparrow?" said yet another waiter, a slight man with a Spanish accent. Paley studied him quickly and waved him away.

"Andie, you think you have me all figured out, don't you?" he asked.

"I have no illusions about my powers of deduction," she said, "but I do have an occasional eye for human nature. And you happen to be human, in case you hadn't noticed."

This talk was setting Paley on edge. Where was that martini that Andie had taken from his hand?

"And I'll tell you something else," Andie said. "You're scared. You're scared your friend was right. You're scared that you're next. It's not guilt that's driving you crazy. It's simple fear."

"You're nuts," said Paley, laughing anxiously. *"Bloody* nuts, as you would say."

"No, I'm bloody *right*," she said. "Fear. We have it over in the British Isles, too." She leaned in close. A rich perfume filled Paley's head, the beat of the bass rose through the floor, and Paley wanted more than anything to be drinking his martini.

"Miss Sparrow, is everything okay?"

Paley glanced away from Andie's face and studied the waiter, a man with shaggy red hair.

"No," Paley said. He looked over Andie's shoulder in the direction of Millicent and Dexter Flamm and the bouncer, and he nodded his head. Then he looked back to Andie, hard. "No, everything is not okay."

The Extra Credit Question is:

How Did Paley Know This Was the Waiter?

(Solution on next page)

∫olution

While the waiter stood there, bewildered, Paley waved over Millicent and Dexter and the bouncer.

"Here's your man," said Paley.

"Yeah, how can you tell?" Millicent asked with obvious skepticism.

Paley turned to the bouncer. "You said you were sure no guest who was not on the VIP list had gotten past you into this room."

"Right," the bouncer answered.

Paley next turned to Flamm. "And Millicent said the name on the note wasn't anybody on the VIP invitation list."

"Right," said Flamm.

"And," Paley said to Millicent, "you also said it wasn't anybody on the invitation list at the door to the club."

"Yes, yes," she said. "We know all this."

Paley ignored her impatience. "So who does that leave?" he asked the group.

"People like yourself," said Andie. "A guest of a guest."

"Right," said Paley. "Only he can't meet Dexter

unless he gets into the VIP lounge. But he can't get in because the bouncer is checking the guests' names at the door. So who does *that* leave?"

"A waiter?" said Andie.

"Right," said Paley. "But not really a waiter. A waiter who's really a guest."

"All right already," said Millicent. "The suspense is putting me to sleep. Let's say you're right. Let's say it *is* a guest dressed up as a waiter. How can you prove it?"

"That's why I wanted to see the waiters here," said Paley. "I mean right *here,* in this corner of the room."

The red-haired waiter stood silently throughout this discussion, shifting from foot to foot. Paley threw him a look, as if to say: *Don't worry. This will all work out.*

"The waiters, I assume, use a service entrance when they come to work?" Paley asked Millicent.

"Of course," she said.

"So that means," said Paley, "that a real waiter *wouldn't have his hand stamped at the door.*"

All eyes in the group focused on the back of the red-haired waiter's hand. And sure enough, in the ultraviolet light, the image of an "X" glowed purple.

In the heat of the moment, the "waiter" admitted that he'd gained access to the lounge precisely as Paley had said: He'd gotten in the front door as the guest of a junior executive at Whiplash Records, then sneaked into the staff area and lifted a uniform from a hook.

"I'm sorry," said the fake waiter. "I didn't mean any harm. I just wanted you to hear my music, Mr. Flamm." He pointed to the cassette in Dexter's hand. "It's a song I wrote called 'The Ballad of Ruth.' It's biblical, from the woman's point of view. . . ."

Paley took Andie aside and whispered to her, "Maybe you could help the guy out. He seems sweet."

"What do you want me to do, take him around the park in a limo?" she asked.

"No, just ask Flamm if he'll listen to the demo tape. Who knows, maybe it's good. Maybe he'll be the next . . . Andie Sparrow."

Andie smiled. "God forbid."

"And while you're at it," said Paley, "could you make sure that Millicent doesn't fire him? I wanted to clear things up here, not get anyone canned. I think Dexter and Millicent will listen to you. After all, you're a celebrity. You've got that . . . je ne sais quoi."

"Enough," said Andie. "I'll be delighted to help out."

Later, when all the business of the evening had been finished, after Flamm had slipped the demo tape into his jacket pocket and grudgingly agreed to give it a listen, and Millicent had disappeared back into the darkness of the club, Paley looked past Andie and over to the table where she had placed his drink. But the drink was gone, long ago cleared away by a waiter or a fairy godmother; the only trace of it was a wet ring on the tabletop. He smiled ruefully, then realized that somehow he was already beyond the moment of temptation. He and Andie stepped out of the lounge, out of the club, and then back onto the dock. As the waiting ferry carried them toward the lights in the distance, Paley felt weary and terrified and inexplicably hopeful, like an immigrant nearing the final leg of his journey.

Chapter Eight
A NIGHT WITH THE HERZOGS

DAVY Herzog was not the jumping type. He was many other types: the Star Trek geek type, the occasional porno movie type, the sweaty-palm type, and the socially graceless type, but he was definitely not the jumping type. Paley just couldn't see Herzog taking a last look around his apartment, swinging one leg up over the windowsill, then the other. Why in the world would a man kill himself, Paley wondered, if he was so worried about being killed by someone *else?*

"Why, indeed?" Belinda asked.

They were having dinner at Fung's All-Night Noodle Parlor, and over sizzling plates of shrimp chow fun Belinda and Paley mused about Herzog's unfortunate death. Paley was out of his funk; slowly it had lifted, ushered along by the pep talk from Andie, and beneath it was an incessantly roiling, questioning mind that wanted to figure out exactly what had happened to poor Herzog.

"It just doesn't make any sense," said Paley. "It doesn't add up." He skewered a shrimp with his chopstick and lifted it to his mouth.

"I agree," said Belinda. "Yesterday at work I was trying to concentrate on some syndication deal my father's been cooking up—something that will keep Beaver Cleaver nine years old well into the twenty-first century—"

"Even better than cryogenics."

"—and all I kept thinking about was Herzog. *Herzog.* I mean, I never even met the guy and already I'm thinking and talking about him as if I know him."

"Must be my brilliant powers of description," said Paley. "Positively Nabokovian."

"Positively Shavian."

"Positively Fourth Street."

"Enough with the jokes." Belinda held up her hands. "You were talking about Davy Herzog, about how you're puzzled by the case."

He nodded; a "case" is what it had become. "It just doesn't figure," Paley said, "Davy Herzog as a suicide." But if Davy Herzog *wasn't* a suicide, then what was he? The second household accident among the Mental Midgets in as many months, in defiance of astronomical odds? A murder victim, the latest casualty in some bizarre conspiracy against a group of maladapted geeks remembered by nobody but Mrs. Cellini and, maybe, a curator at the Museum of Broadcasting? Paley couldn't blame Rose for her lack of enthusiasm about the coincidence of the two deaths. He'd been calling her regularly, describing Herzog's theories in detail, trying to find out what the police were planning to do, and she had been polite, sympathetic, as reasonable as ever; she had assured him that Herzog's file was being processed along the proper channels. And what else could Paley expect? To her mind, the "case," such as it was, was closed.

"Don't eat that," Belinda was saying.

"What?" Paley looked up. Belinda reached over and plucked from his hand a small, dried hot pepper that he'd unthinkingly begun to nibble. Just as he realized what he'd done, the tip of his tongue began to feel as though it had been branded. Paley downed a pitcher of water and waved his hand in front of his face and coughed profusely. Nearby, an entire table of diners turned their heads to look.

"Sorry, folks," Paley said when he was fine again. "That's the end of the show. If you want to watch a Heimlich maneuver tonight, you're going to have to go elsewhere."

Belinda reached across the table and held his hand. "You know what I think?" she said softly.

"I always want to know what you think."

"I think," she said, "that you should go see your friend Rose. In person." Paley raised his eyebrows. "I know," continued Belinda, "you're surprised, right? Because I've been needling you about your relationship with Rose and everything. Well, I'm putting all of that aside. I'm being magnanimous."

"You say magnanimous," Paley sang softly, "I say monogamous . . ."

"I'm serious. I think you've got to go and make her listen to you. And Paley, although you're not great on the phone, you certainly can be persuasive in person."

Paley felt enormously relieved; Belinda was on his side about Herzog, she wanted him to follow his hunches. It made him feel suddenly, unaccountably, happy. "Let's get the check," he said, and he waved for the waiter. Tonight, he and Belinda would watch a movie, would lie close, would make love in the half light of the television. Tonight, he and Belinda would stay inside the little chalk circle that lovers draw around their conjugal beds.

Tomorrow, he'd go see Rose.

But first, Paley had to save some lives. When he phoned Fly-By-Night at seven on Wednesday morning from Belinda's, Candida gave him instructions to report to the New School, where he was to assist a doctor who would be teaching a course in "emergency life-saving techniques."

"Could you be more specific?" he asked.

"That's all I know," said Candida. "But I'm sure it won't be terribly taxing. You sound worn out."

"I am," he admitted. He could hear a rustle of paper over the phone, and then Candida muttered to someone, "Sorted mail, six letters." Paley paused. Was Fly-By-Night's mail already sorted and delivered so early in the morning? It didn't make sense. Then he smiled. " 'Gigolo,' " he said to Candida.

"Pardon me?"

"You're doing a crossword puzzle, right? That's what you were muttering about. And the clue was 'sordid male,' and the answer is six letters long. So it's 'gigolo.' "

"You never miss a trick," said Candida, laughing. "Have fun today. Hope that doctor manages to save your life. We need you around."

So Paley set off down Seventh Avenue on his Braithwaite while the sun was still burning a haze off the city; he wolfed down breakfast at a Greek coffee shop in the Village, where he reflected on his upcoming assignment with some amusement. Still, it was a grim amusement. It was a grim morning; it was a grim day; it was, Paley noted as a pair of slippery eggs stared back at him from his plate, even a grim breakfast.

The job, it turned out, required Paley to play dead—or nearly so. Actually, the doctor running the class told Paley that each demonstration would end with his pulling through; this was the point of the course, after all. As she described the various life-threatened poses Paley would be asked to strike in the course of the two-hour seminar, Paley thought he might have known her from somewhere. Dr. B, as she'd introduced herself to Paley, wasn't beautiful in the classic sense; still, Paley thought

her unmistakably handsome: square shoulders, undisci-
plined black hair, broad jaw, front teeth that overlapped
in a way Paley found fetching. Her manner was matter-
of-fact, her instructions were commendably jargon-free,
and her grip, when she first shook Paley's hand, struck
him as confident but not overbearing. If Paley did ever
need to be brought back to life, he hoped it would be by
someone with hands like hers. Altogether she seemed
the kind of presence that wouldn't be easy to forget.
But apparently Paley *had* forgotten her. It wasn't until
the dozen adult students had scraped together a circle of
plastic chairs and she had donned her lab coat that
Paley got a look at her name tag.

"Dr. Dora Bunyan," he read out loud. She turned to
face him, and for a moment she seemed to waver. One
of her hands fluttered at her cheek, and then she pointed
to him.

"Oh, of course," she said, laughing. "I should have
remembered you when you introduced yourself. Jack
Haley."

"Paley," Paley said.

He hugged her, hesitantly; He wasn't sure how she
would handle this specter from her past. He wasn't sure
what he would think of this specter from *his* past, either. It was Dora Bunyan, missing Midget, the quiz kid
who had been booted off the show after the pilot episode. After all these years, where could they possibly
begin to catch up?

Paley started with the obvious. "I suppose you've
heard about Larry Kelleher and Davy Herzog."

"Yes," she said, shaking her head slightly. "I saw
the obituaries. Such a shame." She gripped one end of a
conference table and started dragging it across the floor.

"You know, I've always wondered whatever became
of you," Paley said. He lifted the other end of the table
and helped her carry it. "We all felt terrible about how

you were treated, all of us on the show. It was so unfair." They set down the table in the circle of students. "It must have been hard."

"Medical school was hard." She smiled at Paley. "Now lie down on this table, please."

"Or maybe I shouldn't even be bringing up the past— after what happened to you."

"Oh, that. That was so long ago."

And of course, it *was*. Since Paley had last seen her, she'd been through medical school, and from the ring on her left hand Paley saw that she'd gotten married, too. She had a career, a spouse, and judging by this class, a commitment to community service. Already Paley could sense this conversation receding into her past. Maybe she would mention it tonight at dinner to her husband, an anecdote she would relate once and then forget, one of those chance Manhattan encounters that come along every so often to remind you that where you've lived all your life is, after all, only an island.

Paley climbed aboard the table, and before long Dora Bunyan, M.D., was pressing her mouth to his.

After spending the morning lying prone, being probed, and pretending he was choking on a chicken bone while Dora grabbed him from behind, made a fist just below his rib cage, and squeezed, Paley welcomed the simpler pace of a police station. He walked down the corridor of the Eighth Precinct, rapped on the frosted glass of Rose's door, and waited.

"Yeah!" Rose called, and Paley took that as permission to enter. Inside, Rose was deep in conversation with two men who looked at Paley through hooded lizard eyes that matched their amphibious leather jackets. Their nervous fingers played on the desktop, their skin was roughed up by old acne. Gold chains glinted under shiny shirts imprinted with scenes of tropical life. Drug dealers, Paley decided.

"I'm just finishing up here," said Rose, not looking up.

Paley stood uncertainly by the door, whistling under his breath and glancing up at her bulletin board. Next to the various telephone numbers of prosecutors and parole officers, Rose had tacked up aphorisms from Malcolm X and Abbie Hoffman. Paley looked back at her. She was a tough cop, but she was also an articulate divorced woman who believed in *causes,* who had spoken to Paley at length in this office of her idea of heroism—people who are patient for change, willing to inch along day to day, doing what they can **do.**

So help me, he wanted to tell her now as he stood in her doorway. *Help me find the killer of my childhood friend.*

"Bargaining with the devil?" Paley asked when she'd ushered out her guests.

Rose smirked. "Not quite, wonder boy. Those are two of our best undercover officers, if you must know."

Paley flopped into a chair. "Touché. I guess I'm a little distracted lately. So," he asked, "are you going to use them on our case?"

She looked puzzled. "Pardon?" she murmured.

"Davy Herzog. My friend who got too friendly with a window."

Rose tilted her head, then without saying a word stood and began rifling through the files that were piled high in a wire basket on her desk. She finally found the right one, flipped it open, and slid it across the desk. "Read," she ordered.

It was Davy Herzog's file. It included a few graphic photographs of Herzog in the repose of death, his body a collection of right angles. Paley stared at the photographs, feeling something deep within himself start to well up. He suppressed it. He read the accompanying text, which was a paragraph long and merely listed the time, date, and location of the death and described the bodily injuries in medical terms. There was a space marked CAUSE OF DEATH; someone had typed in, "Fractured neck after fall from fourth-floor window; apparent suicide." Paley read the words several times before he looked up with anger.

"At least it says 'apparent.' At least you'll give me *that* much. That's mighty big of you."

Rose just shook her head. "Paley, when are you going to see that I'm not 'giving you' anything? I admit you've been helpful to me in the past, but this is not 'our case.' This happens to be one case that has nothing to *do* with you."

Paley sucked a breath between his teeth. "I find that hard to believe," he said quietly. Paley had tried to listen to Rose over the last few days, had tried to dismiss Herzog's death as one more random tragedy in a city full of the inexplicable. But he couldn't do it. He knew Herzog too well; he'd seen sides to him that few others had. He could remember the endless games of "I Confess" that the Midgets used to play in the green room: Larry had been afraid of mice, Tracy had had a serious crush on Samantha from "Bewitched," and Steve sometimes had to wash his hands ten times in succession before he felt clean; Paley had confessed that he had once stolen a box of dog yummies from a store, just for the hell of it—his family didn't have a dog. But none of them could confess like Herzog; he would admit to his crippling fear of vampires or of enclosed spaces, and then the tears would start. The Professor would have to rush poor Herzog back into makeup while the other Midgets sat in silence, impressed by the depths of Herzog's terrors. His fears controlled him in a way that, even then, the others must have suspected they would never fully comprehend. And now Davy Herzog's life had ended exactly the way he had feared it would—in screaming solitude, in violence. And Paley couldn't just leave it at that; such an end wasn't acceptable.

"Please," he tried, "trust me. I knew this guy; he wouldn't take his own life. Suicides don't call up old friends and claim they're afraid of murderers."

"Would you say he was an unhappy man?"

Paley paused. "Well, that depends on your definition of unhappy," he hedged.

"What about friendships? Did he see people regularly, or would you say he spent a lot of time alone?"

Paley again paused. "I don't see what this has—"

Rose cut him off. Her voice was elevated now. "Davy Herzog was not a happy camper! He lived in a dark, cramped, and illegal apartment full of science fiction novels and dust balls! He was deeply unhappy; you can see it in the way he lived. Paley, look, we are not trying to thwart your efforts here. It's just that a murder investigation is a very costly thing, and the police choose to open such an investigation only when there's a reason. And reasons aren't the same as hunches, even yours."

"Don't you think it's odd that two of the original six Mental Midgets have died within weeks of each other?" Paley asked, trying to stay calm. "That neither one died from natural causes? And don't you think it odd that I'd alerted you in advance to the possibility that Herzog's life was in danger, and the next thing we know, he's dead?"

Rose shook her head. "No. You're perceptive, Paley, but what you picked up on was that your friend was in trouble. And indeed he was—emotional trouble. His life *was* in danger. By talking about it the way he did, he was asking for help. I feel terrible that we got there too late, just terrible, but there was no way we could have known."

When she was done talking, Rose began idly fingering some papers on her desk, and Paley took this as a cue. He stood.

"Don't go poking into it," she said without glancing up. "It's police business. You're not authorized, and I can't keep looking the other way for you. In fact I won't. Like it or not, my first responsibility is to provide a reasonably stable environment for my daughter—which includes having a mother who can hold down a job."

It didn't seem like a time for good-byes, so, after a brief but excruciating silence, Paley stepped into the hallway. He didn't look back; he just kept walking toward the exit, through a world of clattering typewriters and outraged voices. At the end of the hall, just as he was pushing open the heavy fire doors, he heard his name. He turned.

"And for God's sake be careful!" Rose shouted to him from the doorway of her office.

As Paley strode into the lobby of the office building where Herzog had lived, he realized that Rose was right. Herzog's life was far from normal. Paley was reminded of the night he'd walked Herzog over to his building after their drink at O'Shea's; he remembered how difficult it had been for him to guess the secrets of Herzog's unorthodox living style. If he was ever going to recreate the circumstances of his friend's death, Paley suspected, he was going to have to start thinking like Herzog—an upsetting prospect at best, an impossible task at worst, but necessary in any event. He would have to start pulling together everything he knew about Herzog; he couldn't afford to overlook even the most random memory from their shared past. After all, this was the same information that had propelled Herzog toward his paranoid conclusions, and if those conclusions proved to be correct, this might be the same information that had propelled a killer toward Herzog.

Paley boarded a waiting elevator and was almost immediately distracted. As the doors opened onto the fourth floor, the first thing he noticed was a smell. Boiled eggs? he wondered. The nearer he drew to Herzog's door, the more pungent the odor. While riding his bicycle uptown from Rose's office, he'd wondered what illegal activity he would have to commit in order to break into the office that Herzog had converted to an apartment: jimmying the lock, taking the door off its hinges, making up some lie for the guard in the lobby? But no solution had seemed appropriate. The one thing that hadn't occurred to Paley was that the apartment would be open, and that someone would be inside.

He pressed his ear against the door. *Voices.*

"So when will it be ready?" a man called.

"What do I have, six hands?" came a woman's reply. "What am I, Vishnu? It'll be done when it's done; I'm chopping celery."

Paley was puzzled. He knocked lightly. In a moment, there were footsteps, and then the woman's voice, just inches away, said, "Who's there!" phrasing the question like an accusation.

"I'm a friend of Davy Herzog's, who lived—who used to live—here," said Paley. Had new tenants moved in so quickly? But that didn't make sense; this was an office building, and the landlord wouldn't knowingly choose to rent to a couple who would bring along a hot plate.

Bolts were slid and the door opened. Paley stood facing a short, squat woman brandishing a spatula. Paley stared at her, knowing he had seen her before, yet unsure where. Then it hit him: She was Herzog's mother. Years before, during the run of the "Mental Midgets," when all the mothers sat in a corner of the studio as required by law, knitting or reading or—like Mrs. Paley—sipping vodka from a flask, Mrs. Herzog would set up a card table and uncomplainingly play solitaire for hours on end. Sometimes, after the director called for silence, Paley could still hear the *slap slap* of Adele Herzog's well-worn cards.

Now a much older version of that woman stared at Paley through harlequin glasses. "Don't I know you?" she finally asked.

He nodded. "Jack Paley," he said in a sober voice, and her face lit up.

"Oh, my," she said. "Oh, my." She shook her head, her eyes filled with tears. "Al," she called. "Al, come here."

Herzog's father appeared behind her, heavy in an undershirt and loosened pants, clutching a newspaper. He quickly buckled his belt and looked embarrassed. "I was lying down," he explained. "It's been a hard couple of days."

"You remember Jack Paley," said his wife. "One of the Midgets, the one who sat to Davy's left." Her husband appeared unsure. "The *tall* one," she said, and finally his face widened in a bleak smile of recognition.

"I'm so sorry," Paley said. "I don't know what to say."

"Come in," said Mrs. Herzog. "There's egg salad."

So Paley found himself having dinner with the elderly, grief-stricken Herzogs, eating off a couple of file cabinets in a dim room where cockroaches moved sluggishly along the inside of an empty watercooler. Paley and the Herzogs sat and talked about the old days, about what had happened to Larry and Olive and Steve and Tracy.

"You were all such adorable kids," said Adele Herzog. "Cute as a row of buttons. I remember the way that pretty Olive could reel off the lists of the planets in order of how much a human would weigh if he lived there, going from most to least. And that nice boy with the Italian name, he certainly knew his vocabulary." She shook her head. "And Davy, he could tell you everything you ever wanted to know about electronics."

"Once," said Al Herzog, "as a prank he hooked up the remote control on our garage door so that whenever you pressed it, the telephone rang. His mother and I would be sitting in the car, pulling out of the garage, when the phone would ring and we'd shut off the engine and race into the house. But no one was on the other end! This happened a few times, until he finally confessed to what he'd done. Davy couldn't live with guilt too long. It just ate at him." He shook his head. "And now he's dead. Our only son."

After an appropriate silence, Paley said, "I know this is difficult, but I have to ask you something." The couple looked at him nervously. "Are you convinced Herzog's—I mean, *Davy's*—death was a suicide?"

They both seemed to flinch at the word *suicide*, then looked to each other for guidance. Finally Adele spoke. "Our son was very special," she said carefully. "Unpredictable. A genius. But moody. He takes after Al that way."

"I'm very moody," Al corroborated. "There are whole *years* when I get up on the wrong side of the bed. 'Sixty-two was like that."

"But more than moody," Paley persisted.

"Well, he did take things so seriously," said Herzog's mother. "He would get all wound up in a project, and if it didn't work out right, he would practically turn blue. And he had ideas about people."

"Ideas?" Paley said.

"Oh, you know, like two weeks ago," Adele said. "He called up sounding depressed and saying he missed us. This wasn't the first talk like this we'd had with

Davy. We always encouraged him to get out more, to go on dates. To live it up in New York." Here she paused, speaking with difficulty. "But of course he was welcome to come down to Florida and visit, if that would help. We even offered to send him a ticket, but you know how Davy was about planes." She paused, dabbing at her eyes. "Not just planes; lots of things. When he was six he went on a class trip to the Children's Museum, and he refused to go inside the human eye with the other children. His teacher wrote us a note, saying that Davy had some kind of . . . what did she call it, Al?"

"Retinaphobia," said her husband flatly.

"That's it," said Adele. "But we knew better. It was part of a whole pattern. Even *elevators* he couldn't stand. Every day he walked up the four flights to get to this apartment. In an office building no less! Illegal! The landlord said we have to move his belongings out of here in three days so a chiropractor's office can move in. Anyway, we really hoped that Davy would come home to Florida and rest for a while, but he said no. The next thing we knew, someone was calling up to tell us he was dead."

"It was like being hit over the head," said Al. "We were stunned." He began to cry softly. "And the thing was, he was our son and we loved him, but he was different from us. And I guess in a way we never really knew him. Never knew what made him tick."

Paley agreed. "When you say he had ideas about people, I know what you mean. I always thought that Herzog had a kind of intuition. Some ability to see the truth that everyone else would miss. Do you know what I mean?"

Adele and Al nodded grimly.

"I hadn't seen Davy in years and years," said Paley, "but I remember how anxious he was all the time. And when I saw him again at Larry's memorial service, he seemed pretty much the same. Then I saw him a second time, and he told me he felt his life was in danger. That's an upsetting thought, I know, and I wouldn't be bringing it up unless I felt it was necessary. That's why I came here today. I don't know what I expected to find. But I'd love a chance to look around." He paused. "I know you feel terrible and I know you just want to spend some time in your son's apartment alone, but I just want to see what I can find. Things don't quite fit. I don't know; a lot of times Herzog was wrong about things. But a lot of times he was right. And I can't just leave this alone until I know for sure. Unless, of course, you insist."

There was silence for a moment, then both Mr. and Mrs. Herzog shook their heads. "No," said Adele, "you're a smart fellow. I remember how you'd answer those chemistry questions when you were nine years old. You'd get a look in your eye. Like nothing else in the world mattered. Like you saw something nobody else could see. It's the same look Davy would get." She stood and picked up Paley's empty plate. Then she stopped and stared at him evenly. "It's the same look you've got now. I trust you. See what you can find."

So that was how Paley came to spend the night dismantling Herzog's apartment. He'd gotten more than he bargained for when he vowed to think like Herzog. Where to start? There was so much to go through in this rat's nest of an adolescent boy's bedroom, years and years of things saved for either sentimental or lazy reasons; it was difficult to tell which. Why would someone save a box of Bazooka bubble-gum wrappers? And what about *TV Guide*s from 1966? "The Mental Midgets" wasn't even on the air then. Was it really necessary to know what time "Mission: Impossible" or "Green

Acres'' were aired more than twenty years before? Apparently, it was.

If there was anything that seemed remotely like *evidence,* Paley picked it up and put it in a pile. His criterion for evidence was any item that seemed less than three years old. And that narrowed the field considerably: He ignored the *TV Guide*s and the collections of Earth shoes and erector sets and the "Star Trek" fan-club newsletters and the comic books, and instead he added to his pile a crisp-looking road map of the tristate area, an address book, and a 1987 tax return. Herzog's parents were sleeping on the cot on the other side of the apartment, and he could hear both of them gently snoring. Paley was exhausted, but the night was young and he had plenty to do.

At four A.M., eyes narrow with exhaustion, Paley began to flip through Herzog's address book. He found listings for a couple of comic-book stores, for the Song Lo Jujitsu Academy, and for several local restaurants that delivered. Paley closed the address book, unsatisfied. Next he picked up the road map and unfolded it on his lap. It was clearly a recent map; the paper hadn't yet taken on the feel of flannel. Paley's eyes surveyed the huge page. On first glance he saw nothing unusual, and he began to fold the map back up. But as he did, he noticed something in the bottom corner of the page: a line drawn in red Magic Marker. He followed the line with his finger, let it lead out of the heart of Manhattan and into New Jersey. Once in Jersey the line led to a town called Burden. And in the heart of Burden, the red Magic Marker made a furious circle. Paley's pulse raced with the excitement of a twelve-year-old boy's discovering a treasure map. *Burden, New Jersey.* Why was the name familiar? He had been to New Jersey dozens of times in his life: to visit friends, to attend weddings, to go on a school field trip to a nuclear power plant. But

Paley didn't think any of his trips had taken him to Burden. Still, the name nagged at him dully. He turned the word over and over in his mind, unsuccessfully. Across the room Adele and Al Herzog slept on their son's cot, rolled together in the middle of the sagging mattress, sleeping the labored, openmouthed sleep of bereaved parents. The sound made Paley start to feel tired as well, and the next thing he knew, he was dozing on Herzog's linoleum floor, the map unfolded over him like a blanket.

Burden. Paley's eyes snapped open; the room was dim with the first morning light. He had been dreaming, and in his sleep he was looking at a newspaper clipping. The clipping was an obituary, and that was when Paley knew where he had seen the name Burden, New Jersey. It had been listed in a real obituary, that of Larry Kelleher. It was where Larry had lived and died.

Paley sat up. Why in the world would Herzog have a map with instructions to Larry Kelleher's house? At Larry's funeral, Herzog had claimed that he hadn't been in touch with poor Larry since they were children. It just didn't make sense.

Actually, there was one way that it *did* make sense, but Paley dismissed it out of hand. This theory, which was absolutely preposterous, went like this: Herzog had bought a map and drawn out a route to Larry's house in order to kill him. Maybe there was some old grudge against Kelleher, some old unresolved jealousy; it was unclear. But after committing murder, Herzog had writhed in guilty agony for months, disguising it as fear that someone was trying to kill *him.* Finally, unable to bear living with his terrible secret, Herzog had taken his own life. After all, Al Herzog had said over dinner that his son never *could* stand to live with guilt. Even when he had rewired the electronic eye in the garage to make the telephone ring, it had been excruciating for him to keep secret his small, innocuous act. If he had that much trouble with a garage door, imagine what he must have felt about a murder.

Paley stood up. His back ached from sleeping on the floor. It was six A.M., and he had pulled together a crackpot theory of murder and suicide. It couldn't be true, he thought, *could it?* He glanced over at the daylight coming through the window, the same window that Herzog had tumbled from. Rose had been certain the death was a suicide; what if she was right? There had been no motive for suicide, but now suddenly Paley was holding a motive in his hands. Maybe there was a very clear connection between the deaths of the two Midgets. He folded the map back up, slipped it into his back pocket, and regarded the Herzogs, slumbering fitfully yet innocently. Let them have a little more sleep, he thought. He didn't want them to wake up yet and ask him if he had stumbled across any clues. *Yes,* he would have to say, *your son may have been a murderer who committed suicide.*

Paley silently let himself out of the apartment. The day was just beginning, and he knew where he had to go.

The two men, student and mentor, sat on a bench in Gramercy Park. The Professor had lived in one of the buildings that ringed the square for as long as Paley had known him; so had Margaret Hamilton, the actress who played the Wicked Witch of the West in *The Wizard of Oz*. When Paley had come here as a child with the Professor, he had often seen her strolling along the paths as if she were just a person, as if she belonged here—and as someone who was entitled to own a key to the park merely by living in this neighborhood, she *did*. The park had served as a retreat whenever the Profes-

sor sensed that one of his charges was slipping. Occasionally Paley would resort to guesswork on the program,
or fail to examine a question closely enough to arrive at
an answer that he did in fact know, and the Professor
would tap him on the shoulder as soon as the red light
had faded from Camera One.

"The park," the Professor would intone, and Paley
would nod sheepishly. A simple lack of knowledge never
brought on such an excursion. Not knowing the capital
of Tunisia was regrettable though acceptable in the Professor's opinion, just as long as you knew it the next
time around. What wasn't acceptable was faulty—or
lazy—reasoning. Not being able to figure out that the
time in Tunis when it was noon in New York City—
assuming that you could figure out from the city's name
that it must be the capital of Tunisia, and that you knew
the country was located on the northern perimeter of
Africa, and that you could safely assume that its nearest
neighbor across the Mediterranean must be Italy, and
that you knew that Italy shares a time zone with most of
western Europe, which you already knew to be six
hours ahead of New York City—was six P.M., was
unacceptable.

"You're not applying yourself," the Professor would
say to Paley as he unlocked the gate to the park, and
another lesson in logic would begin. To this day, Paley
couldn't pass the park without thinking of those afternoons with the Professor, a student and his mentor lost
in a private landscape where the Wicked Witch of the
West strolled, where the only thing that mattered was
knowing how to think. And it was to this paradise that
Paley retreated when he was forced to consider the
possibility that Herzog had killed Larry Kelleher and
then killed himself.

"I need your help," he'd told the Professor over the
phone.

"Where shall we meet?" the Professor said, not missing a beat, even after all this time, and even though it was barely eight in the morning. But Paley couldn't wait. He had left Herzog's apartment and stopped for coffee at a diner, killing time until what seemed a reasonable hour to call the Professor.

"The park," Paley said.

Paley thought he heard an exhaled breath then, a breath the Professor had been holding for fifteen years. Paley reflected back on the Professor's speech at Larry's memorial service, to how sour and sad the Professor had sounded. How many times had the Professor longed to hear the words *I need your help* from anyone, let alone from one of the students he was supposed to have been molding into the rocket scientists of tomorrow? And how many times over the years had Paley longed to call the Professor, but had stopped himself before picking up the telephone? After all, he hadn't *done* anything with his life yet, and he was embarrassed and afraid that he had let the Professor down.

"Of course, Paley," the Professor said now, his voice low and thoughtful, "of course."

As soon as Paley had locked his bike outside the park gate, they slipped into old patterns. As Paley outlined everything that had happened over the previous weeks—including Herzog's paranoia, Rose's insistence that Herzog's death was a suicide, and the marked-up map—he and the Professor made circles around the perimeter of the park. Throughout Paley's explanation, the Professor remained silent, hands shoved deep into pockets. Even when Paley told the Professor that he was starting to wonder if Herzog had killed Larry and later killed himself, the Professor said nothing. It was only when Paley was done talking and they had arranged themselves on the very same wrought-iron bench where they used to meet that the Professor looked at Paley and nodded once.

"And that's it?" the Professor asked.

"That's it."

"So where's your problem?" the Professor asked kindly. "Why did you get me out of bed so early on this fine morning? It sounds to me like you've figured everything out on your own." But there was a note of whimsy in his voice, as though he were enjoying a secret joke.

"My problem," Paley said, "is that I don't really believe what I'm saying."

"No? What about it don't you believe?"

"Well," Paley began, and he wasn't sure what he was going to say until he said it, "if Herzog had murdered Larry—and I'm only saying *if*—then why would he go through all the trouble of convincing everyone that Larry's death *wasn't* a household accident? Why did he make everyone start thinking about murder and risk implicating himself?"

"An interesting question," said the Professor. "So interesting that you ought to spend a little more time on it, I suspect."

"I've spent time," said Paley impatiently. "I've been thinking about nothing else all morning. But I keep coming up against the same wall. Herzog said he hadn't been in touch with Larry Kelleher, but that was obviously a lie, because there was a map to Larry's house in the bottom of his closet. Why would he lie unless he had something to hide?"

"I don't know. But what I do know is that you should consider your question. Carefully."

"What do you mean?"

"Well, you've made a certain assumption."

"I have? What assumption? Where? It seems straightforward to me."

"An oval track seems straightforward to a horse wearing blinders," said the Professor.

Paley almost laughed. "All right. I'll take it one step at a time. I'll go back and think some more. I'll go back to that greasy spoon where I had breakfast this morning and I'll plop down in a booth and think until I've figured it all out."

"Sometimes," said the Professor, "there is something better than *thought*. Not often, but sometimes."

What was better than thought? Paley wondered. He leaned forward on the bench, his head in his hands. This was a lot easier, he thought, when the only thing at stake was figuring out what time it was on a faraway continent. Now what was at stake was the honor of his friend—which, after all, was what Herzog had become to Paley, even if Paley would never have the chance to tell him so—and the safety of the remaining Mental Midgets. Paley felt a chill pass over him, a gentle reminder of mortality. A long silence passed while the two men watched a young girl on a skateboard float by.

What was sometimes better than thought, Paley finally thought, was action.

"I've got to go," Paley said.

The Professor smiled slightly. "I thought you might say that."

"Do you know where the nearest car rental place is?" Paley asked.

But the Professor was already holding out a set of keys. "It's an '82 Volvo. Brown, sunroof. Radio gone. Copy of *The Aeneid* on the dashboard," the Professor was saying. "Takes a little warming up, but she shouldn't give you any problems. The garage is on the corner of Madison and Twenty-eighth. Just have it back before nightfall."

Paley reached out to hug his old teacher. "I can't

thank you enough. You've really been so helpful. Just talking about it made it easier.''

"Paley," said the Professor, "one more thing."

"Yes?" Paley hefted the set of keys in his hand, eager to take off.

"I spoke to Herzog."

"When?"

"Last week," said the Professor. "He called me. I didn't know how much to take seriously. You know how David could be."

Paley nodded. "We all got those calls. All the Mental Midgets heard from Herzog."

"As you just said, he went on and on about how everyone's life was in danger. And how his own life was in danger." The Professor paused. "But there was one more thing." He took a breath. "He said he knew who wanted to kill him—and I didn't pursue the point. I just let it go." His voice broke. "And now I can't stop thinking about it." He rubbed his eye with the palm of his hand. "I should have listened. I should have listened to Herzog. Goddamn me to hell, I should have listened. Once in all these years one of you comes to me and says he needs help, and what do I do? I throw it away. I cast him aside. I can't even be bothered to listen."

"To what?" Paley whispered. "Listen to what?"

"And now he's dead. Two of you, dead. I never wanted to see this day. I'd always thought I would be the first to go. You can't know how much I never wanted to see a day when I would still be walking this earth and you, my wunderkinder, my life's work, would be gone."

The Professor was crying silently now. He buried his face in his big hands. Paley leaned closer to him and put his arms around him. But after a moment the Professor pushed himself away.

"And that's not the worst of it," he said in a new, rough voice.

Paley didn't respond. He didn't want to hear what was coming next. It was almost as if he knew what it would be, what it had to be, just as Herzog must have known. At some moment the truth must have pierced Herzog just as it was now pinning Paley to a bench where he had spent countless afternoons as a child, in a park that Paley knew he would never again pass without thinking of this moment, a place that he would never again recall as heaven on earth.

"He said it was one of you," the Professor said.

The car drove beautifully, if you liked cars. Paley did; he had a secret love of cars, in fact, and whenever anyone asked him if he liked to drive, he always nodded vigorously. Some of his love of cars, though, had to do with the fact that he never had to drive one. There was nothing romantic about driving a car in Manhattan, Paley realized as he approached a bottleneck outside the entrance to the Holland Tunnel. Cars were standing still even though the light was green. Drivers leaned on their horns and let them rip, as though loud, flatulent sounds might get results.

Herzog's map, which was spread open in Paley's lap, gave directions to head through the Holland Tunnel and into New Jersey. Paley considered taking an alternate route, heading uptown to the Lincoln Tunnel or the George Washington Bridge; but he reminded himself that the purpose of this outing was to do what the Professor had encouraged him to do—to take action, and to learn from his actions. What was there to be learned today? Paley wondered. Supposedly, Larry Kelleher had been alone in the house the day he died. No one had reported seeing anyone enter the house, but it was possible that Herzog had parked the car elsewhere and slipped into the house unnoticed. Anything was possible.

The line of cars entering the tunnel was endless, and Paley kept shifting back into neutral as he sat. Finally he was next, and he went from bright daylight into the dim, tiled glow of the tunnel. Traffic picked up speed, and Paley began to enjoy the ride. He thought about many things as he drove: Herzog's messy apartment, his collections of gum wrappers and old shoes. Paley and Herzog as boys, playing the riddle game. But when he tried to think about Herzog as a killer, or Herzog as a suicide, it just didn't compute.

The tunnel seemed to go on forever in rows and rows of tiny yellow lights. But then, just as the tunnel ended, and Paley was back out in the open daylight of a New Jersey afternoon, something occurred to him. He was so overcome that he swerved sharply and pulled into a Gaseteria without signaling. Paley got out of the car and walked shakily over to a bank of telephones, yanking clumps of change from deep inside his pockets. His heart was racing, but he was *relieved*. To his left, cars zoomed by, continuing on into the towns and cities of New Jersey—businessmen and women, commuters, shoppers, vacationers. Everyone had a reason to go to New Jersey.

But not Davy Herzog.

Paley dialed the number of Rose's precinct.

"I've got some news," Paley said.

"Where are you?" Rose said. "You sound like you're in the middle of an expressway."

"Fresh out of the Holland Tunnel, in a filling station in New Jersey."

"I suppose it's too much to hope that you're simply going for a drive in the country and not digging into the Herzog case."

"I know what you're going to say. But listen to me first."

"All right, Paley. But make it fast. I'm busy."

Paley allowed himself a moment to catch his breath. Then he quickly explained to Rose about the map he'd found at Herzog's apartment. And he explained how he'd thought that Herzog might have killed Larry Kelleher and then himself.

"But Herzog didn't kill himself," Paley said.

"No?"

"No. Because he didn't kill Larry Kelleher."

"What?"

"And I think I can prove it."

The Extra Credit Question is:

How Did Paley Know?

(Solution on next page)

∫olution

Paley explained to Rose how the Professor had urged him to take action. "So that's what I did. I drove through the Holland Tunnel."

"I know. You're in Jersey. The Garden State. Land of Springsteen. You already told me."

"But that's just it," Paley said. "As kids, the Mental Midgets had played a game called 'I Confess,' where we told our biggest secrets. Herzog's was that he'd always been terrified of enclosed places, and I know he never got over it. He was so phobic he lived on a low floor in his building so he wouldn't have to use the elevator. He wouldn't even get on a plane if you gave him a free ticket. When he had a choice of taking a bridge, Herzog would never have planned a trip for himself that involved *going through a tunnel*."

"You might be on to something."

"So somebody must have planted that map to make it look as if Herzog killed Larry," Paley said. "And then killed himself, out of guilt."

"But who?" said Rose.

"I think I know. And I think it's time the Mental Midgets had ourselves a little reunion."

The Extra Credit Question is:

Who Did It?

(Solution in next chapter)

Chapter Nine
ЛHOWTIME

IF it hadn't been for the sign in the hallway outside, Paley wouldn't have recognized Studio B. Somehow, he'd expected to find the old set of the "Mental Midgets" show intact, like the bedroom of a child who has died long ago and whose parents can't accept it. He'd expected to find the single row of six school desks and the Professor's lectern, and next to that, a blackboard and pointer. Under the hinged top of each desk there would be three No. 2 pencils with points as sharp as needles and a thick pad of scratch paper, ready to be fanned and sniffed and, finally, scratched on.

Instead, what Paley found in Studio B was a carnival ride. It took him a moment before he recognized it as the set of "Crash Course," a game show in which teenagers in bumper cars were tested on their knowledge of TV trivia. Paley had tried watching it once but had to turn it off; the sight of three slack-jawed thirteen-year-old boys unable to come up with the name of the president who had once told a nationwide TV audience that he was not a crook was too much to bear.

By the time the others arrived, Paley had done his best to re-create a reasonable facsimile of the "Mental

191

Midgets" set. He'd pushed the bumper cars into a corner, pulled six folding chairs out of the wings, and set them all in a row, right in the center of the stage, exactly where they used to be. The studio was huge; back during the "Mental Midgets" days it had been the jewel in the network's crown, a state-of-the-art marvel that in one day could house "Uncle Wicky's Morning Wonderland," a full week's worth of tapings of the game show "Swing Your Partner," "The Bix Joplin Talk Show," and of course, "The Mental Midgets."

Now, beneath the huge "Crash Course" video monitor, Paley had placed a table that would have to serve as a makeshift lectern; beside it he'd rested a huge sketch pad on a music stand, a sort of makeshift blackboard. And then he'd simply taken a seat in the chair that would have been his—last one on the end, stage left—and waited.

From this chair Paley couldn't see past the cameras and into the audience. All he saw was a wall of white light; it was all he'd ever seen up here. The Professor would ask a question, the studio audience would hush, and Paley would sweat and stare, like an animal hypnotized by headlights. Afterward, everyone would tell him how relaxed he'd looked, and Paley was always surprised that his true feelings hadn't showed, that sweat hadn't beaded on his forehead and made his pancake makeup stream down his neck and into his black graduation gown.

Paley felt that same anxiety now. Just as the broadcast had been unrehearsed and live, so tonight would he have to live by his wits. Over the last couple of days he had discussed his hunches with the Professor, and together they had set up the reunion of the Mental Midgets. Even at this moment, the Professor was probably down the hall in the lobby, gathering the ex-Midgets together. Paley wished it could be a Tuesday, the night they'd come to Studio B in the old days. But what Paley hoped to accomplish tonight couldn't wait. Arranging for the studio on a Sunday night was the easy part; all it took was one call to Belinda, who collected a few favors from her well-placed contacts at the network.

"Can't I go with you to the studio?" Belinda asked when Paley explained his plans. "I think I ought to be there, Paley. It's not going to be easy."

But he shook his head. They were in her bathtub at the time, two disembodied heads having a conversation. Underwater, their limbs lightly touched. "No," Paley said softly. "I don't think you should come."

"Oh, you and your Mental Midgets," said Belinda. "You're so secretive about it, so protective. I feel like I have a boyfriend in Skull and Bones, or the CIA."

"There's a difference?" he said, but Belinda didn't smile. "I know, I know. You feel left out, and I hate it. But bear with me, Belinda. Just once more. Let me do what I need to do. I've just got to take care of some unfinished business. It won't be long."

Beneath the water, she grabbed his foot and held it, as if to say, *Be careful; you belong to me.*

Next Paley had paid a visit to Rose. He stood before her desk and delivered an impassioned speech that he'd rehearsed endlessly, and she stared back at him in silence. He outlined his suspicions. He explained his intentions. He anticipated her objections. Finally he ran out of things to say.

"So," he said, "what do you think?"

"I think I must be crazy," she answered, "but I trust you. What do you need?"

"Two of your finest," he said, and she agreed. Now the officers waited out of sight down the hall, outside Studio B.

Inside Studio B, it was showtime.

*   *   *

"I have a feeling," he heard Tracy's voice intone, "we're not in Kansas anymore."

Paley looked up. She was the first to enter the circle of light; one by one the rest of the Midgets emerged from the darkness, like survivors of a tornado stumbling outside and checking the skies. They fanned across the studio, picking their way through the cables that snaked across the floor, blinking into the arc lamps.

Paley stood up, stepped forward, and said, "I guess this is the part where I should say something like, 'You're probably wondering why I've invited you all here tonight.' "

Everyone laughed, out of politeness more than anything else. "Well," Olive said, "there *is* something vaguely creepy about this. I mean, I can understand wanting to get the old crowd together, but isn't this a touch dramatic?"

Paley said nothing. He saw Steve walking around and surveying the place. "No chips or dip?" Steve asked. "What kind of party are you throwing, anyway?" He shook his head. "I gave up a hockey game for this, Paley, just because you said it was important."

"It is," Paley said.

"Don't get me wrong, I'm as nostalgic as the next guy," Steve went on. "I mean, just walking into this building again gave me goosebumps. Or coming down that corridor there. Or even seeing the sign that says 'Studio B.' Especially that."

Everyone nodded in agreement. Paley himself had felt a definite tingle—a whole series of them, actually—starting the minute he walked into the building tonight; it was like a string of firecrackers laid out along his spine. He thought about how he had stood in this circle of light for the first time as a seven-year-old boy with his whole life ahead of him, fielding question after question, and how he stood here now as a fully grown man.

"Say, everyone," the Professor said, clapping his hands. "I've got a little surprise. Paley was feeling kind of sentimental and wanted to have a reunion, and he asked if I would put together some questions, like the old days, but just for fun. So I've written up a battery of questions in each of your areas of expertise. I thought we could play a round."

"Yeah," said Steve, sidling up to Tracy, "let's play around." Tracy rolled her eyes.

"I don't have a lot of time," Olive said, glancing at her watch.

"Ah, time, what is time?" the Professor asked. "Perhaps Steve can answer that one."

Steve put his hands behind his back, tilted his head to the ceiling, and said, *"Time.* Definition: The measured or measurable period during which an action, process, or condition exists or continues. *Time.* Alternate definition: A continuum which lacks spatial dimensions and in which events succeed one another from past through present to future."

The Professor smiled. "There we go. Some things never change." He shook his head. "If only my students were one-eighth as bright as you," he said sadly. "Ah, well." He waved a pack of index cards. "Shall we get this show on the road?"

With some embarrassment and a good many jokes, everyone took a seat. The two empty chairs were conspicuous. Paley remembered the way Larry would sit straight up at his desk, alert and impetuous as a puppy, and the way Herzog would slouch like a delinquent. He felt his throat tighten at the thought. But this was no time for sentiment.

"Maybe I can catch the end of the hockey game if you let me out of here soon enough," Steve said. "Hint, hint."

Tracy shook her head. "I think you're going to have to perform first," she said.

"Isn't this adorable," said Olive. "Reliving old times. How sweet."

The Professor stood behind the makeshift lectern and shook his head. "Didn't any of you have any fun back then, answering questions and showing the world how gifted you were?"

"*Were* is right," said Tracy. "It's just hard, Professor, remembering the way we were."

" 'Mem'ries . . . ,' " sang Steve in a startlingly nasal voice.

"But the way you were," the Professor continued, "was wonderful." He paused, picking up an index card. "Tracy," he said suddenly, "here's something in your category, Geography. The hour is noon, eastern standard time. What time would it be in Addis Ababa?"

"Twenty hundred hours," Tracy answered promptly.

"Correct. And in Caracas?" the Professor said.

She paused. "Thirteen hundred hours."

Everyone was rapt. The spell had taken hold, the tension rising as questions were fired and answers tentatively or boldly offered. How in the world did Tracy know all the things she knew? It really was a marvel, Paley thought. It was a marvel that all of them had their own distinct skills, their own particular pockets of obscure knowledge that in the real world no longer counted for anything. But in here, in the heart of Studio B, knowledge was everything.

"Correct. And in Karachi?" the Professor asked kindly.

"Twenty-two hundred hours."

"Correct. . . . Let's do just one more. Please give me the correct time in Vladivostok."

Tracy's face blanched. She looked away from him, squinting out into the darkness as though the answer might be revealed there. Paley knew that she was trying to picture the international time zones, the jagged boundaries that sometimes conformed to longitudes and sometimes not, and to do a little quick math at the same time. Finally she swiveled her head forward and said to the Professor in a bold voice, "Oh three hundred hours."

The Professor stared back at her, silent for the longest moment. Paley could feel waves of tension in the air.

"Oh three hundred hours," Tracy said, "the *following* day."

"Correct!" the Professor finally said.

And everyone spontaneously clapped.

Now the group seemed to be getting into the spirit of the evening. Paley was called on next, and even though it had been his idea to arrange the whole event, he felt anxious as the Professor threw difficult questions his way. "Paley's category, as you will all remember, is Chemistry," said the Professor. "I thought I'd ask him a few questions regarding the discovery of some of the less obvious elements."

Paley swallowed hard. He could hear his blood pound inside his head.

"Let's start with the element holmium," said the Professor. "Please tell me the name of its discoverer and the date of discovery."

"Holmium," said Paley, then he licked his lips. "Uh . . ." He searched his mind, that bottomless shopping bag of facts. "Soret and Delafontaine, 1878."

"Correct. . . . Yttrium?"

Paley paused. "Gadolin, 1794."

And so on. The Professor asked him half a dozen such questions, then began asking the city in which the particular element was discovered as well. And even though it was enormously difficult, Paley rose to the occasion. If you've once had a passion for a subject, a true love and understanding of it, then the information will stay attached to you forever. He closed his eyes and let the atomic elements dance before his eyes, as they did when he was trying to fall asleep at night. The answers flowed.

"Correct!" cried the Professor at the end of the inquisition.

Then it was Steve's turn to be asked about word derivations. Steve leaned forward, chin resting in his hands, and spoke eloquently on the origins of *puerperium* and *chalcedony*.

Finally only Olive was left. "Now," said the Professor, "we'll ask Olive a few puzzlers about her beloved subject, astronomy."

Olive stared, unblinking. "I've got to get home soon," she said.

"Come on," said Steve, "we've all been put on the spot. You can do the same."

"Yeah," said Tracy. "You always used to love to flaunt your knowledge of nebulae and asteroids."

"Yes, well," said Olive, "I'm shy about it now."

Steve started to laugh. "You may be many things, Olive, but you certainly aren't *shy.*"

The Professor smiled. "Shall we proceed?" His voice had a firmness about it that Paley had never heard before. "Olive, I'm going to name some planets, and I'd like you to tell me their sidereal periods of rotation. We'll begin with Mercury."

There was a long pause, and then Olive said, "No." Her lips were compressed into a line.

"Think of it as an initiation," Steve said. "Kind of like rush week in a fraternity."

"But what fraternity *is* this?" Olive asked. "The Brotherhood of the Geek?"

"The doomed geek," Paley said softly, looking at the two empty chairs.

Nobody spoke for a moment. Then the Professor said, "Do it in memory of Larry and Davy. One last time. Come on, answer the questions, Olive."

She stared at him. "I don't want to play this game."

But the Professor would not relent. "Can you tell me the sidereal period of rotation for Mercury?"

"I forget," said Olive.

"Forget or *don't know?*" said Paley, standing up.

"Forget," snapped Olive.

"Can you even say what a sidereal period of rotation *is?*" Paley asked.

"Please," Olive said in a shaky voice. "Please, all of you, just leave me alone."

But Paley had hardly begun. He thought of the younger version of Olive whom he had kissed in the green room so many years before, of the girl whose braid had come undone in his hands. But that was another Olive, he thought. And that Olive was gone.

"Do you want to explain why you don't know anything about astronomy?" Paley asked.

But Tracy interrupted. "What are you saying? Olive was brilliant when we were kids. Especially about astronomy."

"Astrology, maybe," said Paley. "But not astronomy." He shook his head. "Olive's been faking her way through life for a long time."

"Preposterous," said Steve. "She's a whiz. She knew the night sky as if it were the back of her hand."

"Well," said Paley, still not taking his eyes off Olive, "she must not look at her hands very much. Or maybe"—his voice lowered—"she's been too busy doing something else." He took a deep breath. *"Like pushing Davy Herzog out the window."*

"Paley, do you know what you're saying?" Tracy cried.

Paley nodded. He could feel his fluttering heart. Belinda was right; this *wasn't* easy. It was terrifying, but he managed to keep talking. Soon it would be over, he reminded himself. Soon it would all be over.

"I tried to put everything together, but it just didn't make sense," he said, moving up front to the lectern. The Professor stepped aside. "The obvious thought," Paley continued, "was that someone had killed Larry Kelleher. And that the same person who killed Larry wanted to kill Davy Herzog. I couldn't get this idea out of my head. It was Herzog who put it there in the first place. I started thinking about who would have a motive to bump off the Mental Midgets. While I was trying to figure it out, I just happened to run into Dora Bunyan— you remember her. 'Poor Dora' we all called her. And as soon as I saw her I thought: Now there's a motive; now there's someone who would certainly feel a ton of anger toward her past. But frankly"—he shook his head— "Dora Bunyan is in much better shape than any of *us*. She's hardly *poor* at all. She's got her act together, she's a respected doctor, she has a life that gives her satisfaction. She barely *remembers* the days of 'The Mental Midgets.' " Paley paused. "So then I thought of Olive."

"I was in England when Larry Kelleher was killed," Olive said quickly. "I can prove it; I have receipts from Harrods."

"It doesn't matter." Paley smiled tightly. "Herzog was only half right. He was right to think his own life was in danger. But he wasn't right about Larry; Larry's death, as far as I can tell, *was* a household accident. Larry had always been a klutz, you remember. It seems that he simply slipped on the stairs leading down to the basement. Nobody killed him." Paley paused. "But Herzog was another story. Herzog *was* murdered, and Olive capitalized on the fact that Davy had been ranting on and on, quite vocally, about a conspiracy to murder all the Mental Midgets. Olive *wanted* Davy dead, and this was a perfect chance to make it seem as though Herzog's rantings were those of a lunatic, and that he himself had killed Larry over some ancient, nerd-boy grudge, and then went on to kill himself out of guilt."

Olive sat perfectly still, her hands in her lap, but Paley's entire body was vibrating like a Magic Fingers machine. It felt extraordinarily strange to stand at the head of the class, delivering this lecture.

"Olive planted a map to Larry's town in Herzog's apartment, hoping to lead the police to think that Herzog had been the murderer. And it almost worked, too. But then I remembered how phobic Davy was about enclosed places."

"I remember that, too," said Tracy softly. "He was so afraid. He'd start shaking if you even *said* the word *elevator*."

"Exactly," said Paley. "He never would have taken a route that forced him to go through a tunnel, and the route on the map did. So I knew the map had been written on by someone else. And that that person was the killer."

There was silence. Paley could hear his voice echoing in the cavernous studio. Suddenly he felt chilly, even under the hot white lights. He rubbed his arms. "After I figured this out, I thought about something the Professor had said. He told me that Herzog had suspected it was *one of us*. And I thought to myself, which one of us would have made such a clumsy mistake as the tunnel business? Then it struck me: The mistake wasn't clumsy; it was just a mistake. There was only one of us who never sat in on those 'I Confess' sessions when we were kids. And that one of us was Olive. She was always slightly apart from the group. She was usually off with her mother and Tony Minion. We all got to know each other very well except for Olive. And it just stands to reason that if Olive is still the unknown one among us, then she is also the *least knowledgeable* about everyone else. So she never knew about Herzog's phobia. She drew a map that had him going through a tunnel. Which is something that no one else among us would have done."

"But why?" Steve burst out. "Why would she do this? She had no reason."

"That's what I couldn't figure out, either," said Paley. "It just didn't make sense to me. Why would she commit murder—Olive, who had everything going for her, who was brilliant, who was beautiful?"

Olive looked up at Paley, blinked once, then lowered her head again. Paley went on.

"Then I remembered something that had happened back at Larry Kelleher's memorial service. It had seemed small and insignificant at the time, and I had barely thought about it since, but as I tried to fit all these weird pieces together, somehow this memory came back to me. At the memorial service, when we were all standing around on the steps, Herzog said a harmless thing to Olive. He leaned over and said something like, 'I know a secret about you. A *big* secret.' I'll never forget her face when he said this. She went dead white." Paley paused, staring at Olive. "In fact, she was about as white as she is right now."

Paley took a long swallow from the glass of water on the lectern. "Later, I asked Herzog what he had meant by saying that, and he told me that he had just heard, through someone he knew at MTV, that Olive was going to be given her own television show. Every day Olive would wear a miniskirt and answer difficult questions, stuff like that. The news hadn't been announced publicly yet, but Davy had the scoop. He was only teasing Olive about it."

"And that's enough for her to kill him?" Tracy asked, folding her arms across her chest. "I don't buy it."

"You're right," said Paley. "It's not enough. The sad thing is, Olive didn't *know* that that was all Herzog was talking about. She thought he knew something much, much worse about her. Something that could cost her the show. Something that could ruin her reputation forever."

"And what was that?" Steve asked quietly.

"That she wasn't the world's smartest woman," said Paley. "Not even *close*. And that she had *never* been particularly gifted, not even when she was a Mental Midget. Because she became a Mental Midget by less than scrupulous means." He shook his head. "Remember how the Widow Herne—I mean, Olive's mother— used to pal around with Tony Minion all the time? Well, you may have read in the papers that Olive's mother married Tony Minion after the show went off the air. But what you didn't read was the fact that Tony and Mrs. Herne were lovers well *before* the show went on the air. And that the only reason Dora got bumped from the program, and Olive got on, was because of this connection. And worse yet, Tony illegally fed Olive answers throughout the entire run of 'Mental Midgets.' "

There was silence. Paley stared straight at Olive. "You know nothing about astronomy, never have," he said, though his voice wasn't unkind. "And very little about history or geography or linguistics. It was all a scam, and no one ever found out. Then one day, fifteen years later, your life is going great and you're about to have a hip TV show of your own, and along comes wormy little Davy Herzog, and he whispers something to you, and you think he knows your awful secret! You think he wants to ruin you! So what do you do? . . . You kill him. You go up to his apartment and probably pull a gun on him and back him up against the window. Maybe you give him a nudge. Or maybe you tell him he has to jump or you'll kill him. So he jumps. And because Herzog lived in an office building, where thousands of people come and go through the doors every day, no one could possibly identify you."

Paley wiped his brow with the back of his hand, then he looked around at the faces. He saw that Tracy was gently crying, and that Steve looked stunned. Even the Professor, to whom Paley had explained everything in advance, sat with his head in his hands. Olive was staring at Paley.

Suddenly Olive stood. "You think you're so smart," she said in a low voice. "You all do, but you're just a bunch of misfits. You're all geeky brainiacs without a life, and you make me sick with your 'areas of expertise.' Your boring word derivations. Your stupid atomic elements. What was so wrong with my wanting to be like you? To be special? So what if I had a little help? It was worth it, to get the recognition. To have people respect me. To have people think I was *somebody*. Everything was wonderful when I was twelve years old. I wish I could be twelve again." Olive moved swiftly as she talked, and in a moment she had slipped out of the spotlight and into the darkness.

"Wait!" Paley called, striding after her across the shiny, dark studio floor. He looked right and left, but couldn't find her; had she just disappeared? But then he heard her crying and saw that in a corner of the studio, Olive had climbed into one of the bumper cars from the set of "Crash Course." But the car was built for someone much smaller, much younger. Olive sat with her knees up at her chin, weeping.

"Olive," Paley said quietly from several yards away. The acoustics were such that his voice came out clear and he didn't need to shout. It had always been this way; back during "The Mental Midgets," when Paley had wanted to answer, he had simply lifted his head, looked into the camera, and spoken softly. "The atomic weight of gadolinium is one fifty-seven point two five," he had said, and everyone had applauded.

Now Paley stepped forward and gently helped Olive out of the bumper car. He put his arm around her and together they walked across the dark studio, toward the EXIT sign. The two police officers who had been discreetly waiting in the hall now moved forward, taking Olive by the arms. She did not resist. For a moment Paley considered accompanying Olive and the arresting officers to the precinct. He watched as Olive was led down the hall, past the door that had once opened on the green room, all the way to the elevator. But then Paley heard a sound, and he turned to find the remaining Midgets and the Professor standing in a shaken, bewildered huddle behind him. He needed to go back to them now.

Paley leaned against the door of the studio, waiting for someone to speak. Tracy went first. "How did you get conclusive evidence that Olive had been fed answers?"

Paley smiled sheepishly. "I didn't. But I just had a hunch about it. I mean, here's this woman whose entire career hinges on her being so brilliant. Here's a woman who is known just for *being* brilliant—not for having done anything with that brilliance. And when I started thinking back to the beginning of the Mental Midgets, it suddenly seemed really peculiar that Dora Bunyan—who knew everything under the sun—was bumped so unceremoniously for Olive Herne. I asked myself why would Tony Minion be so dead set on having Olive on the show, and the answer was: because her mother wanted it. And then I asked myself: Doesn't it seem a little odd that Tony Minion, who's producing a show about child geniuses, just *happens* to be having an affair with the mother of a genius? The most logical conclusion I could draw from all of this was that it was a setup, a fake, that Olive was simply a pretty girl with a good memory, and that every week before the broadcast Tony Minion and the Widow Herne supplied her with all the answers she'd need to deliver on Tuesday night."

"But why would you think Olive would believe you had conclusive evidence about any of this, when all you were going on was a *hunch?*" Steve asked.

Paley smiled slightly. "Well, for one thing," he said, "she's *not* the world's smartest woman."

Later that night, after they had all said their drawn-out, emotional good-byes, hugging each other just a little harder than they might have imagined they would, and then gone off to their separate lives, Paley retrieved his folded Braithwaite from a corner of the studio and caught up with the Professor. Together they walked along the silent street, past porno theaters and gated storefronts and parking lots.

"Well," said the Professor, "you did well."

"Under your tutelage."

"Not really. On your own. You're not twelve anymore, Paley. You don't need a tutor. None of you does."

Paley shoved his hand into his pocket. The thought began to sink in that he was twenty-nine years old, that he was six feet one inch tall, and that he had his own apartment and steady, interesting work and a girlfriend—for want of a better word—who sometimes thought he was terrific.

"Do you think we'll be okay?" he asked the Professor. "Not just me—all of us?"

The Professor didn't hesitate. "Of course. I never had a doubt." He paused. "It was an exciting time back then, working with all of you and doing the show every week. And it's an exciting time for all of you now, too. Finally *getting on with it,* as we say."

Paley smiled. He felt, in that moment, that somehow they *would* all get on with their lives, and that they would continue to check up on each other as the years passed. They no longer required the occasion of someone's death to stay in touch.

Suddenly the Professor looked at Paley and said, "Isn't there somewhere you should be now?"

Paley blinked. "Pardon?"

"Somewhere you should be, someone to go home to," said the Professor. "You mentioned that you have a girlfriend, so I imagine that you would want to be with her on a night like this."

Paley opened his mouth to respond, but stopped himself. How could he explain his Tuesdays-only arrangement to the Professor? He could almost hear himself resorting to the kind of semantic horseplay that at an earlier age would have earned him a stern look from the Professor and a two-word reprimand: "The park." It was as if the mental gymnastics Paley had been performing all evening had exercised some long-dormant muscles. He didn't feel fatigued; he felt alert, renewed, mentally limber. In that moment, Paley realized that the Professor was right: he *did* want to be with Belinda now. He missed her in some profound way that took him thoroughly by surprise.

The two men said good-bye on the corner of Fifty-second and Eighth, then separated before things became too maudlin. After the Professor had disappeared down the street, Paley unfolded his Braithwaite. Then he paused, realizing that it was exactly the time of night when the city was just sinking down into sleep, when any two people who were still awake might feel as though they had the entire island to themselves. Was it really so terrible of him to want to see Belinda tonight? No, he decided, it wasn't so terrible at all.

Steam floated up silently from manholes, neon studded every corner, dark buildings loomed in the distance like dinosaurs. It was stunning, it was heart stopping, but right now Paley didn't have time to stand still and look. This wasn't Tuesday, but somehow it didn't matter. He swung a leg over his bicycle and took off into the street, flying along an avenue where every traffic light glowed green.